THESE LIES

A JACKLYN STONE THRILLER

JACKLYN STONE THRILLERS SERIES
BOOK 4

SUSAN SPECHT ORAM

SOS COMMUNICATIONS LLC

Published by SOS Communications LLC in 2025

www.susanspechtoram.com

First Edition

ISBN (e-book): 979-8-9926053-8-9

ISBN (paperback): 979-8-9926053-9-6

 Formatted with Vellum

PREVIOUSLY

PREVIOUSLY IN:

SHORE LODGE

Jacklyn Stone, a grieving widow and garden store owner, is admitted by her greedy son to Shore Lodge, a secure psychiatric facility. She must escape to rescue her dog and reclaim her home.

BY MIDNIGHT

Jacklyn helps friends gather money to keep a debt collector at bay, but the clock is ticking in a race against time.

THE WINTER STORM

Jacklyn and her friends return to Shore Lodge to free four residents from a secure psychiatric unit on Christmas

Eve. But a storm is brewing, and her devious son is out to thwart her every move.

THE COLD NIGHT

A snowstorm traps Jacklyn and her dinner party guests with her conniving son. When Jacklyn's friend's daughter is kidnapped, FBI agents must find the missing teenage girl.

AVALANCHE

Hearing intruders in her home, Jacklyn grabs a candlestick and charges toward danger, catching her bitter child in an unforgivable act. Her son ignores avalanche warnings, and his wilderness trek turns into a nightmare.

1

ZOILA

I pull on a dress, straighten my wig and step over to a window, gazing into the house next door, where my ex-husband and his new wife live. Kirk is in the kitchen cooking my birthday dinner. It was kind of him to invite me over to celebrate, although I sense his wife isn't as keen about welcoming me into her home. Jenna has been frowning at me and asking questions about my medical condition. I don't like how suspicious she is, so I've come up with a secret plan to distract her from my supposed illness.

Tapping a finger to my cheek, I smile. I'll convince Kirk to invite me to move in with them next door, because I have cancer and need help. I'll settle into their guest bedroom upstairs, right next to the master bedroom, and Jenna will forget her prickly, probing questions. She'll be seething with jealousy by the time I'm through with them.

Tromping down the stairs to the kitchen, I open the refrigerator, and cool air wafts out, making me shiver. I grab a bottle of sparkling cider, slam the fridge door shut, shrug on a winter coat two sizes too big for me and zip it up. The coat hangs like a tent, which is what I intended. I've been throwing up and losing weight to keep Kirk convinced of my medical maladies.

With a nod, I remind myself it won't be long before I can wrap up the ex-husband project, and these lies will deliver the justice I've sought since he jilted me for Jenna. I'm not looking forward to spending my birthday dinner with Kirk's new wife, who is irritatingly upbeat and pleasant, but I head outside and hobble down the front steps, carrying the chilled bottle and leaning on a railing for support, in case Kirk and Jenna are watching out a window.

Cold wind whips past, tree branches sway in a stiff breeze, and I suppress a smile. I'll tug at their tears during dinner and set my trap. When the snare is sprung tonight, they'll invite me to move in with them, and I'll infiltrate their lives, fingers creeping into their finances, prying their lives apart and getting payback for what they did to me. There's no cure for the broken heart Kirk gave me, but when this episode ends, it'll be all their fault for inviting me into their house.

2

JACKLYN

I frown and look up from my laptop, saying to my friend Mercury, who is reading on the couch, "You won't believe what just happened."

He closes his book. "Try me."

"The city water department says I have to pony up and pay for four fire hydrants and a new water line to adjoining properties before I can build my housing development on the hill above town. What a bunch of boneheaded nonsense this project is turning out to be. The hydrants and water line will cost well over one-hundred-thousand dollars and obliterate the budget and cost estimates I turned into the bank."

He tugs on his gray mustache. "Have you considered dropping the project? It sounds like it's been a hassle since day one. Think of all the time you'd have to do something else."

My eyebrows shoot up. "I don't want to do something else, and besides, I can't drop it, because the project meant so much to my husband. He and Dusty dreamed it up."

He's quiet for a moment, and I purse my lips, pondering how to best honor the approaching one-year anniversary of my husband's passing. I'm not sure what to do, but I won't be going out in a kayak to scatter his ashes, braving currents and blasts of cold winter wind. I'll have to think of a better idea in the coming days. I shake my head and marvel at how strange this last year has been, filled with betrayal and family drama, like when my son Dusty tricked me and admitted me to a secure psychiatric ward at Shore Lodge on Cedar Island.

Mercury's soothing, mellifluous voice interrupts my thoughts. "I'd guess your son said something to the planning department people, before he was hurt in the avalanche, to trigger these fresh concerns about your building project. The fire hydrants, water line and environmental survey suddenly came up as new issues and that smells suspect to me. They were never a concern when he owned Stone Construction and Stone Estates was his proposed development project."

I release a long sigh. "You're right, and Dusty does know people in the planning department, having been a contractor for so long. It seems his mission, after his dad died, has been to siphon off my money and throw up roadblocks. Now that he's locked up in Shore Lodge and out of my sight, there shouldn't be any more surprises. He can't talk yet, and I made sure he doesn't have access to a phone or computer there. I know as his mother I should visit him at Shore Lodge, but I'm not ready to face him yet."

Mercury creases his brow, leaning forward. "Only go back to Shore Lodge when you're sure you're ready, because that place shook you to your core, from what you've said. I'd hate to see you visit and stir up past trauma. It might be tough to deal with."

I nod. "The overwhelming feeling of claustrophobia in the tiny isolation room nearly undid me." But I flash him a half-smile and make a pathetic attempt at humor to lighten the dark mood in the room. "It was mop up on aisle nine after that mess, literally."

He cocks his head. "That was a lot of stress for you to handle. Not to mention what happened here at your home, when Dusty staged a home invasion."

I clap a hand to my chest. "I still can't believe my son broke into my house at night with another man. It shook me to my core."

He says in a calm voice, "If I'm being honest, I think Dusty wants you dead and to have all of your money and your house to himself. It's as simple as that, and that's why it's a very good thing he's locked up in Shore Lodge."

A tear trickles down my cheek, and I wipe it away. I loved my son as my flesh and blood, but his actions after his dad died have been reprehensible, adding up to utter madness. He carries a chip on his broad shoulders as big as the mountain he ventured out on recently, when he ignored warming temperatures and almost died in an avalanche.

Mercury gazes at me. "Am I guessing right? Are you upset because your wedding anniversary is coming up?

I swallow, and my throat is parched as an August day during a drought. "The day Albert died haunts me, and I wake up at three in the morning with my eyes wide open, reliving that terrible time, over and over again, in my mind."

"That's the worriers' hour, when we're wide awake and alone with our troubles, reliving past terrors and mistakes we've made."

"I agree, and I know we can't change the past, but the movie of what happened when my husband passed replays in my head. My rusty CPR skills didn't bring him back, and I watched him die. I was powerless." A shiver runs through me, and I cross my arms, aware I'm protecting my wounded but healing heart.

He adjusts a blue bow tie clipped to his long gray beard. "You're one of the most powerful people I know, and you keep overcoming obstacles and making things right. If you're feeling powerless, there's no hope for the rest of us."

I blink back tears. "I was shocked when it happened. We know death is coming, but there it is, poof, right in front of us, all of a sudden. It's one thing to talk about it, but another to see it first-hand."

"Death is a stranger until it's gazing into our eyes and holding our hands."

Thrown back to the moment Albert died on our wedding anniversary, I shudder. "I have a lot to do before I kick the bucket, like building a subdivision and spending time with you and my family."

Mercury smiles. "Sounds good to me."

"I hope Dusty will get better, so he can live on his own and find work. But Nurse Wright at Shore Lodge said he has a long ways to go."

Mercury sits back. "Here's an idea. Why don't you leave him at Shore Lodge, like he did to you, and put him out of your mind? He ruined your dinner party on Christmas Eve. Before that, he put Buddy in a shelter and sold your garden store out from under you, so cut your losses and don't look back. He won't change, or grow into a bigger, better person. I'd say his conniving personality is baked in for the long haul."

I shake my head. "I won't do that. It wouldn't be right, and he has no one else to look out for him. No one cares about him, except for me, and maybe his sister."

He shrugs. "It's your choice, obviously. It's not my family, but I just thought I'd offer an opinion from the outside looking in."

"I appreciate what you said, and I might change my mind in the future, but right now I'm sticking with my flesh and blood."

Feeling restless, I stand and go over to the living room

window, gazing into a dark winter late afternoon. "Something strange is going on down the block with Zoila and Kirk and Jenna. I'll check with Jenna to see what she has to say about it."

He comes over to stand by me, staring into the gloom. "I'd leave it if I were you. Nobody likes neighbors poking their noses in where they don't belong."

I tilt my head, smiling at him. "Are you implying I'm a busybody neighbor?"

He chuckles. "Yes, that's exactly what I'm doing."

I give him a kiss and say, "Don't worry. I'll be fine. I won't get too wrapped up in other people's lives."

3

———

JACKLYN

I wave goodbye to Mercury, as he leaves to have dinner with his new roommate, Del, who understands grief and loss like it's a musical score playing in his head. Del ran from Shore Lodge and joined us on Irena's boat during a Christmas Eve storm, and I admire how he's making his way in the world and starting a new life for himself as a widower. It's not easy, letting go of the past and moving on, as I well know.

My beagle-mix rescue dog Buddy sits and stares at me, waiting for his first dinner, and I bend and scoop up a cup of kibble, pouring it into his bowl. "There you go, sweet dog."

He gobbles down his food, metal tags clanking against the bowl, and I pull out my phone, texting my neighbor Jenna, who lives two houses away. 'How're you doing?'

She texts back. 'Need to talk. Can I stop by?'

'Come over anytime.'

A few minutes later, she knocks, and Buddy runs to the door, barking. I glance out the window, nod to Jenna and open the door wide, gesturing for her to come in. Buddy's tail wags.

She rushes in, wide eyed, and I offer her coffee, tea or water. She shakes her head. "No thanks. I just need to talk to someone before I blow my temper back at home. I can't take much more of this, or I'll go stark raving mad."

I grimace and point to the dining room. "Let's sit in there. It sounds bad."

She takes a seat at the table and says in a hushed voice, "Can I tell you something in complete confidence, and you won't say a word to anyone?"

I perch on a chair, wondering what I'll hear. "Of course. I'll keep my mouth shut and won't tell a soul. What's this about? And can I take your coat?"

She leans in. "No thanks. I can't stay long. I think Kirk's ex-wife is pretending to have cancer."

My jaw drops. "You mean Zoila, my new next-door neighbor?"

She nods. "Yep."

"Why would she do that?"

"For attention and to get Kirk's sympathy and maybe take our money."

I screw up my face. "That's a pretty serious accusation. Are you sure? It would be hard to pull that off and convince people and involve telling many lies."

"It would, but she's slippery and smart. Conniving is her middle name."

"It seems drastic and devious, like something Dusty would do."

She looks around. "Is anyone else here in the house?"

"Nope, just Buddy and me."

She raps her knuckles on the table. "I'm sure of it, and I just have to prove it."

I cock my head. She's normally a calm person, but she's wired tight and unnaturally nervous. "Listen, don't march around making false accusations, because that could backfire on you big time."

She bites her lower lip. "I know. The worst of it is, part of this whole thing is my fault because I acted like it was fine if Kirk had her move in next door. But now she's over all the time, or calling and texting him. It's pretty much constant, and they're too close, but I feel like I can't say anything about it, without looking like the bad guy, since she's supposed to be sick."

I say in a soft voice, "But maybe she is ill."

She clenches her hands. "I'm fed up with her hanging around the house, hugging him for far too long and flirting, laughing at his jokes. Her behavior is over the top, but he doesn't see it that way. I think he's flattered by the attention."

I blow out a breath. "Wow, that sounds like a lot. Is there anything I can do to help?"

She glances at her phone and stands. "Thanks, but

just talking about it helps. I've got to get home. Kirk is making a special birthday dinner for Zoila at our house, but I can't stand being around her, not even for a minute. She's invaded our lives and wiggled in between us, little by little, one day at a time."

I walk her to the door. "Let me know how the dinner goes. I know all about being in close proximity with an enemy after my ill-fated Christmas Eve dinner, when Dusty showed up uninvited and stayed overnight."

She stops on the threshold. "Actually, it would help if you'd happen to walk by during dinner and come join us for a bit. It'd help break up the tension between the three of us. I feel like it's two against one."

I nod. "Sure, I'll stop by with Buddy while we're out on a walk. I can do that." My dog rubs against my leg, and I bend to pet him. She strides out into the wind, and I close the door.

I say to Buddy, "How bad can it be that Jenna thinks she needs a referee? It's only a birthday dinner, for heaven's sake."

Buddy rolls over on the floor, and I scratch his belly. Wind whips past my bungalow, and window panes rattle. I say to Buddy, "It's wild outside, but nothing ruffles our feathers, except for the bone-headed people down at the water and planning departments."

Whooshing out a breath, I feel like I'm climbing a mountain with Stone Estates and getting nowhere. My son Dusty Stone placed boulders in my path on the way to the summit, and time is running out. In the next few days, I must sign for a construction loan at a high interest rate and use my home as collateral, or horror of horrors, ditch the entire project on my property with a view looking west to the San Juan Islands in Washington State. It would be a huge loss if I dropped the idea and didn't go forward, for the town, for future home buyers, and for me.

4

IRENA

My thirteen-year-old-daughter moans on the couch, saying she's too sick to go to school. With a frown, I put a hand on her forehead, wanting to fix what's wrong. My father kidnapped her on Christmas Eve and tried to take her across the Canadian border, but they were turned back. He headed south, intent on hiding her in an abandoned fishing shack along a river, but Kelly fought back at a convenience store off the freeway until the FBI arrived.

I say, "Your forehead feels fine, but I'll get a thermometer, just to be sure."

She groans. "It's my stomach. I told you that."

I cringe. "You need to see a doctor. You've been missing too much school."

She grunts. "I don't need to see a doctor. School makes me sick. No one understands."

"Is it something you ate?"

She turns her head, staring at me. "Why are you asking so many questions? I need to rest."

I sit beside her and smooth her hair, but she turns away. Clearing my throat, I make an attempt at sounding calm, despite turmoil inside. "I called the school and told them you were sick. They asked if you'd be back tomorrow."

Kelly's breathing stops. Her chest doesn't rise. Her hands form fists.

I say, "I told them I wasn't sure, but I hoped you'd be back at school tomorrow."

Kelly says in a tight voice, "I don't want to go to school, not tomorrow, not ever."

I drum my fingers on the sofa cushion, trying to think of what to say. "Did you talk to your counsellor about this?"

She opens an accusing eye. "Yes, but it's none of your business."

I shrug. "Okay, I respect that. Listen, I was planning to go to Buzz's house to take a look inside. Rest here, and I'll be home in a few hours. Get some sleep."

Her eyes flash open. "Can I go too?"

I hope I'm doing the right thing when I say, "Sure, but first we'll stop at your dad's and Abby's place to talk about how you're feeling."

She rolls her eyes and sits up. "Fine."

I rest a hand on my churning stomach, because we're

in for a bumpy ride. I'd heard navigating living with a teen is often fraught with tension, and I thought I understood what that meant. But I had no idea of the turbulence waiting in our choppy household waters. Kelly and I are surrounded by a storm called the teenage years, and it's my job to stop our boat from sinking.

5

———

JENNA, KIRK'S WIFE

I look out the window and watch Zoila making her way down her front steps. Kirk stands by my side and says, "I'll go help her. She looks weak, don't you think? That bottle looks heavy for her to carry. And it's her birthday, after all."

I grasp his hand before he goes. "Before she gets here, I want to say something."

He frowns, glancing toward the front door. "Now isn't a good time to talk. She's coming over for dinner, and I know you're not happy about it, but try to act welcoming. She's going through a tough time."

"Hon, she's fooling you. I don't think she's getting chemo. She's not sick."

He puts his hands on his hips and glowers. "What a cruel thing to say. Ever since she moved in, you've changed and not in a good way. Look at her, she can barely walk. She needs our help."

Shaking my head, I doubt he can see what's right in front of him, but the picture is clear to me. Zoila is putting on an act and taking advantage of him. I clear my throat. "If you'd asked me before inviting her to dinner, I would've said no. I don't want to spend that much time with your ex-wife, who fawns all over you. It makes me feel uncomfortable."

His brows knit together. "It's a little late to voice that, when she's almost here. She's our friend, not just mine."

I resist the urge to roll my eyes. No planet exists where I'll befriend the ex-wife next door who uses her feminine wiles to pull my husband close. She's an octopus, wrapping her tentacles slowly around his waist. She'll devour him for dinner and it won't register with him until she's digested every drop of his affection and energy. She might be draining him of money too, so I need to check the bank accounts.

He open his hands. "Besides, what am I supposed to do? She my ex-wife, and she has no one else to turn to. She needs me. The least we can do is celebrate her birthday tonight."

I cross my arms. "She's pulling your strings and making you dance to her tune."

A knock sounds at the door, and he whispers, "This again? Really? I'm beginning to wonder who you really are. You've been picking fights since she moved in next door. She'll always be my friend, and we'll welcome her into our home for as long as I live."

I raise my eyebrows. "I'm fed up with you putting her first. Pick between us."

He hisses. "This is not the time or place to voice these concerns." He turns away, strides to the front door, flings it open and hugs his former wife. Zoila wraps her arms around his neck and lingers, leaning into him.

Breaking out in a coughing fit, I blame myself for allowing the she-devil to move in next door. But I just need to focus on tonight and make it through the meal. A birthday dinner can't last that long. Buck up, I tell myself. Soon, I'll be soaking in a hot bath, sipping a glass of wine and forgetting she was ever in our house.

Kirk takes her coat, hangs it up and laughs at something she said, slapping his thigh. She tips her head back and giggles, training her eyes on him. My chest grows tight. We're trapped in a game she's playing, and I must find the strength to hold on until she gives up and moves away. If that doesn't happen, I'll have to come up with another plan.

6

KIRK

I hurry to the door, fling it open and hug my former wife. I can feel the frown on Jenna's face without turning around to look. Zoila wraps her arms around me, holding on tight, and I step away to take her coat. From the way her dress hangs down, she's lost a lot of weight. She's thin and frail from undergoing cancer treatments, and I want to do all I can to help her through this difficult time.

Zoila flashes a smile, holding my gaze. "Remember that horrible birthday dinner you made when we were first married?"

I chuckle. "The burnt pizza tasted like cardboard, didn't it?"

We laugh together, and it feels like old times, when all was well and we were happily married. But that was before I met Jenna. I don't understand why Jenna is upset about this dinner. There's nothing to be worried about. I say, "Let's go in the kitchen."

Zoila hands me a chilled bottle of sparkling cider. "I'll stop in the bathroom first. Is it this way?"

She rushes down the hall, closing the bathroom door with a thud. My wife and I raise our eyebrows, looking at each other. Through the door, we hear the sound of retching, and I cringe.

Leaning over to Jenna, I say in a low voice, "She's really going through it. She's pale and puking, and we haven't even eaten what I cooked."

Jenna says, "Don't make it spicy. It might be hard on her stomach. Chemo must be rough on her. A friend from work had no problem though. She just breezed through it."

I swallow and eye my wife, who strikes me as being cold and calculating. She's not the person I married after ending things with Zoila. Water runs in the bathroom and turns off.

Zoila opens the door and grips the door jamb before coming toward us on unsteady legs. "Is there anywhere I can sit down?"

"Of course," Jenna says. "Right this way. We'll sit in the kitchen."

The two women slide onto bar stool seats, side by side, leaning forward with their elbows on the counter. My two partners, past and present, sit before me, and I hope they aren't judging me. I'm not a perfect man, far from it, and

I've made my share of mistakes, like when I left Zoila for Jenna. But I'm trying my best, like tonight, to make it up to my ex-wife by preparing a special dinner for her birthday. Everyone likes a party.

I open the bottle, grin at Zoila and pour her a glass of sparkling cider. "Happy birthday."

I pour two glasses of red wine and hand one to my wife.

Taking it from me, Jenna says with a smile. "Yes, happy birthday."

Zoila takes a sip and sets her glass down, picking at a cuticle.

I lift a lid off a cooking pot. "I made a special dinner for you, your favorite."

She wrinkles her nose. "Is that fish I smell? I can't eat it anymore."

My wife winces. "We should've asked first if you had food preferences or dietary restrictions. I'm sorry we didn't do that."

I nod. "I'm sorry. I'll throw it out and start over. I can cook pasta, if you like."

Zoila puts a hand on her stomach and rushes to the bathroom, slamming the door shut. My mouth falls open, and I say to Jenna, who is scowling, "Guess I called that wrong. Lots of changes since she got sick, too many to count."

Jenna nods. "Yes, too many changes to count."

7

———

ZOILA

I slam the bathroom door, push up the toilet seat and hang my head over the toilet, pretending to puke and coughing. Letting the toilet seat drop down with a thud, I issue a loud moan and flush before washing my hands. I stop and smile to the mirror. Growing up, I wanted to be an actress and tonight's performance is showcasing my talents..

I smooth my dress and slowly walk in the kitchen, where the stove fan is whining, windows are open and fresh air blows inside. Shivering, I cross my arms. "Brrr. It's cold. Do you have a sweater I can borrow, or a fleece jacket? Being cold really gets to me lately, even since I started cancer treatment."

Kirk's eyes open wide. "Of course. Jenna, why don't you get that sweater I gave you for Christmas and give it to her? It be our gift to you. Keep it for as long as you like."

Jenna's eyes flash, and she clenches her jaw, but she covers up her consternation with a shrug. "I'll be right back."

I say, "I'll go with you. I'd like to see the upstairs of your house."

8

JENNA

I clench my hands and charge upstairs, shaking my head. I had wanted a sweater like this for years, and yet he offers it to her? This was my Christmas gift, for heaven's sake. In this crystal-clear moment, I know he's not my ally, because he's taking his ex-wife's side. His love for her is obvious, but until now, I missed the signs.

Zoila follows me, but I ignore her. I yank open a closet and pull the precious knit sweater off a shelf. But I stop in my tracks. I don't have to do what Kirk says and give away my cherished Cowichan sweater that I've wanted since our trip to British Columbia.

Three years ago, before Zoila slithered back into Kirk's life, we took a vacation to Canada and had a blast. We laughed, we played card games, we stayed up late counting the stars from Salt Spring Island. We drank coffee in the mornings at the Tree House Café and watched boats come into the harbor.

Zoila disappears into another room upstairs, and I sit on the edge of the bed, holding the sweater in my arms, and smile. We took the ferry to Vancouver and sipped mugs filled with foamy lattes. I glimpsed a sweater like this in a shop window on Robson Street, but they didn't have my size, and ever since then, I've wanted one.

Zoila appears in the doorway and watches me with a sly look on her face. She glides into the room and reaches out her slender fingers for my treasured sweater, but I tug it out of her hands. No words are exchanged, but this is warfare, I feel it in my bones.

I stand and quickly slip my arms into the sweater, gathering it around me and plastering on a fake smile. "Hang on, I'll get you a different sweater."

She tugs on my sleeve, invading my space. She's close enough for me to smell whiskey on her breath. There's no way she's sick. She's a stinking liar, and I'm going to prove it.

She says, "I've always wanted a sweater exactly like that. Kirk said I could have it for as long as I wanted, so it's mine."

I stride to the closet and hand her a cashmere sweater that itches and makes me scratch my neck. Besides, it's too big for me. "Wear that. It'll keep you warm, and it's soft."

She holds it close to her chest and peers into my eyes.

"You're cold and callous, not like the woman Kirk described when he left me for you. Where's your heart? Don't you care that I'm always chilled from being treated with chemotherapy?"

I blow out a breath. "I'm sorry you're going through this, and I apologize. I'm just jealous that you have so much of Kirk's attention, since you moved in. It must be tough to have a cancer diagnosis and go through treatment. I can't imagine what you're going through."

I reach out and give her a stiff hug, patting her back. She steps back and says, "Thanks for saying that. You don't know the half of it, but I really appreciate you and Kirk helping me through this most difficult time."

We tromp downstairs, side by side, and I bite my lower lip. Slowly but surely, this woman is invading my home, inch by inch, and I want her out of here as soon as possible. Every nerve in my body screams for her to leave and move to a new town, so I can return to my regular life, which was just fine, before the she-dragon named Zoila moved in next door.

In the kitchen, she pulls on the cashmere sweater and twirls around like a child hungry for attention. Zoila throws out her hands and grins at my husband. "Don't I look beautiful in this sweater?"

My husband, the man who is becoming a stranger to me, rushes over and hugs her, patting her back. "Of course, you look beautiful. That's my Zoila."

I turn away and roll my eyes at their over-the-top display of affection. This house is way too small for the three of us, and I can't wait for her to go home.

9

———

IRENA

I drive with my daughter to her father's place and park out front. We hurry to the house, and Kelly says, "I'm curious to see Buzz's house after this. It might be creepy without him there."

I knock on the door. "You're right. It'll be strange being inside his place, and I still can't believe he's gone and left it to me."

She says, "He loved you, Mom, don't forget that."

I swallow, thinking back to when I loved Buzz, until our ship hit the rocks of his deception and lies. Our relationship sank to the bottom of the sea, and no rescue operation could revive what was lost between us.

Jack, my ex-husband, limps to the front door, leaning on a cane and recovering from a traumatic brain injury. He hugs Kelly and holds an index finger to his lips. He lets us inside and points to Abby, who is asleep on a recliner in the living room. Gesturing to the kitchen, he hobbles ahead, and we follow him.

Slumping in a seat at the kitchen table, he reaches out and holds Kelly's hand. "I heard you didn't go to school today and that concerns me, because I love you. What can we do to make you feel better?"

Kelly's eyes fill with tears, and she blinks them away. "Dad, don't make me go to that school. The kids make fun of me, and no one understands what I'm like after what happened with Granddad. I stick out and can't stand being there."

Silence fills the room for a beat, and I say to Jack, "They're gossiping about her. It's pretty hurtful, and I talked to the principal."

Kelly moans, resting her head in her arms. "I told you not to do that. It'll only make it worse."

I sigh. "They said their hands are tied, because no one hurt Kelly physically, and it's all rumors and lies."

Jack cocks his head. "What kind of rumors?"

Kelly closes her eyes. I wait for her to say something, but her lips are pressed together in a tight line. I say, "The school counsellor called me today."

Jack's jaw tenses. "And?"

I shake my head. "Apparently there's a rumor going around school that Kelly is shooting up heroin in the boy's locker room."

Jack's eyes grow wide, and he sits up. "What?"

Kelly jumps out of her seat. "That's crazy and not true.

Wait, they called you, and you didn't tell me about it until now?"

I frown. "I didn't want to upset you, because you were sick. You were sleeping, and the nurse asked me to check between your toes and fingers for needle marks. I did but didn't find anything."

Jack balls his hands into fists. "Tell me who spread these lies, and I'll settle this with them right now."

I pat the table. "I don't think any one person is behind this. It sounds like a group of girls is targeting our daughter. Is that right, Kelly?"

She stares at the floor. "Yeah, pretty much. No one talks to me, not since I was kidnapped. I'm different now, and they put a target on my back."

Jack and I exchange worried glances, and he rubs his forehead, saying, "This is messed up. Their talking behind your back must be getting to you, if you don't want to go to school."

Kelly wipes tears from her eyes. "It is."

"What can we do to help?" Jack says, patting her back.

She leans into him. "Home school me, or send me to Grand Island to live with Tex."

Jack gives me a death glare. "Have you discussed this with Tex and not told me?"

"No," I say. "You're her father. I wouldn't do that."

He says to Kelly, "Your mom and I will talk it over and come up with a plan. Go to school tomorrow before you miss any more homework and classes. We'll settle it by the end of the week, I hope."

I release out a weary breath and rise. "Okay, Kels, let's go see Buzz's house."

She stands, but Jack looks like he was slapped in the face. "Why are you going there? He's dead and gone."

"I'm sorry, that must have come as a shock. Buzz left his house to me in his will."

Jack's jaw drops, and Kelly chimes in. "I got the leather-bound first edition set of Dickens books that I'm never going to sell, according to his wishes."

Jack's shoulders shake. He wipes his eyes and stands, leaning on his cane. "It was a dark night when Buzz hit me and stole my memory, leaving me for dead on a dead-end road. Good riddance. May he not rest in peace, after what he did to me."

I bite my lip and usher Kelly out the door. I don't think she needs to hear vengeful talk like this. We're trying to knit her together after her abduction, and Jack's reaction isn't helping my cause. We say goodbye and stride out to the car.

Heading to the house I inherited, Kelly turns to me and says in a tight voice, "I understand why Dad is angry about what happened to him, but he's got to get over it."

I slow our speed and turn a corner. "Why don't you talk to him about it? You both went through trauma that blew up your lives. You could support each other."

She says in a quiet voice, "That sounds corny, and not like a club I want to join."

I pat her leg. "I know, sweet girl, I know."

We're silent and keep our thoughts to ourselves, while I drive the remaining blocks to my former boyfriend's place. Either Buzz changed or his true self came out when he hit his best friend Jack in the head and left him for dead. I should get t-shirts made saying, "I survived when Buzz went bad." Or, better yet, "Don't trust him with your heart. Report if seen. Danger lurks, and he's armed with books."

My mind drifts back to when Buzz and I were in seventh grade, and we hung out at the library after school doing homework. He was as close as my third arm back then, and look at us now, torn apart by life and death, truth and lies, and his leaping off Jackson Bridge, never to be found.

A mix of muddled emotions makes my stomach ache, and I pull up outside his house, wondering what we'll find inside.

10

———————

KIRK

While Jenna and Zoila, the two bookends of my life, are upstairs getting a sweater, I fill a pot with water, set it down on the stove and turn on the burner. Shaking my head, I blame myself for not realizing fish odors might affect Zoila when she's sick. I should have asked what she wanted to eat, but I assumed she hadn't changed, which was my mistake. Was it wrong to dump Zoila to marry Jenna? I followed my heart, wanting to flee from a plotting partner who demands more from life at any price than it gives her. Although I upgraded to an even-tempered, happy wife in Jenna, she's been out of sorts lately.

I rummage in the pantry and pull out a box of pasta noodles. We'll have a simple, bland meal, because my planned feast failed. My armpits are damp with sweat, and I wipe my forehead, wondering what is taking them so long upstairs. Gnawing on my lip, worries churn in my gut, because deep down, I fear Zoila harbors a vendetta. She may act sweet to me now, but I have an underlying sense she's secretly out for revenge.

Wiping my brow, it occurs to me that bringing together the two women in my life for dinner might blow up in my face, because I don't want my ex-wife telling Jenna about my past misdeeds. But Zoila and I came to an agreement, and as long as I pay her medical bills and rent, she won't tell Jenna that I took from the till and moved money to my personal bank account at the first place where I worked. I was young and didn't know better, or at least that's what I tell myself when I look in the mirror.

Water simmers in the pot, and I chew on the inside of my cheek. I shouldn't have stolen from the hot tub business, or let Zoila, my wife at the time, know I did it. In the wee hours of the morning, I recall what I did, and my eyes flash open. I stare at the ceiling, wondering what was wrong with me that I stole money in my early twenties. We needed a car that didn't break down, and Zoila suggested I take cash from where I worked. They'd never miss it, she told me. Gus, the owner, was like an uncle to me, clapping me on the back when I sold a hot tub to a happy couple I knew from high school, but I went ahead and stole from him. I never should have done what Zoila wanted, because that put me in a pickle, and now I'm being squeezed by Zoila, who knows my secrets. She has the power to ruin my life. I escaped her clutches by divorcing her and moving to this small town, but she tracked me down a few months ago and called me at work, telling me what I must do to protect my past.

Bent over my computer at work, I was entering numbers in a spreadsheet for my job as accountant for a plumbing supply company, when the phone rang. I answered and to my horror, Zoila was on the other end of the line.

"Hello," she said in a soft voice. "Did you miss me? You tried to escape, but I found you."

I gulped and looked around to see if anyone could hear me talking on the phone. "Hold on." I got up, closed the door to my office and picked up the phone. Sweat trickled down my arms. "How did you get this number?"

"It didn't take much, just a little sleuthing. Now that you're a big-time accountant, you're about to help me out."

My hand trembled holding the phone. "Listen here, leave us alone. We moved to Millersville to start over. Don't call me again."

"Don't forget who you're dealing with," she said. "I know what you did. Do you want everyone to know and lose your cushy job? When your secret comes out, you'll go to jail, and Jenna will leave you."

I swallowed. "No, I don't want that."

"Listen up, and listen close. You're going to find me a place to live, right next door to you."

My eyes darted around, not seeing anything. "What? I can't do that."

"Yes, you can. Tell the neighbors in the cute house next to you to take an extended vacation, and you'll pay for their trip in exchange for me living there rent-free."

I shook my head. "There's no way they'll go for that. They have jobs, and I can't afford it. It's crazy to talk about this. It'll never happen."

"Make it worth their while and pay them rent. I know you can pull it off. You're smart and devious, like me, but people don't know that side of you. The other thing is, I was diagnosed with cancer."

I frowned. No wonder she was upset and back in contact. "Oh, I'm sorry to hear that."

"The problem is, I don't have health insurance, and I can't pay for treatment and doctor's appointments. I need you to foot the medical bills while I go through this."

My mouth hung open. "I'm sorry, but this is too much. I can't help you."

"Yes, you can," she said. "You'll find a way to pay for all of it. Because otherwise, your life will become an open book, and they'll arrest you for what you did."

I release a sigh, realizing I must comply with the wishes of the devil I divorced. "Fine, I will. How long will this go on?"

"I'll be getting cancer treatments for a year, maybe longer. Look, here's my number. Call me as soon as you get your neighbors moved out, and I'll move in. We'll be one happy family."

She gave me her number, and I jotted it down. My

hands trembled, and the writing was jagged. How did she weasel her way back into my life? I must protect Jenna by telling her lies and keeping her away from Zoila's poisonous grasp.

It's always been all about Zoila, in Zoila's mind, including the day I married Jenna. We went out to dinner, just the two of us, to celebrate. We settled into seats at an Italian restaurant, candlelight flickering as we held hands and I ordered two glasses of prosecco. The waiter brought them, and he grinned when I said we'd just gotten married.

I raised my glass. "To my new bride. I love you."

Jenna smiled and raised her glass, but just then, Zoila pulled up a chair, sat down and said, "I've heard him say that before." She turned to Jenna. "Who knows, you might get tossed out and someone will take your place, like what happened to me."

Zoila reached over, took the glass from Jenna's trembling hand and drank it in one gulp. "I don't wish you both health and happiness. I hope you wake up one morning and realize you made a mistake by marrying each other. And one day, Kirk, you'll wish you'd stayed with me. I see that clearly in your future."

Jenna's eyes grew wide. "Get out of here and leave this instant. Don't ruin our wedding day."

Zoila leaned in, flashing cleavage from her low-cut red dress, one she wore on our last anniversary dinner. "Jenna, tell me why you did this to me. How can you live with yourself, knowing you snatched him away from another woman's arms? A woman who loved him and would've stayed with him until the end." Zoila wiped a tear from her eye.

Jenna tapped a fingernail on a water glass. "All I know is hearts can change. He loves me now, so please, find a way to deal with it and move on with your life. The three of us won't be having friendly dinners together. We're moving away and starting over. You won't know where to find us."

I cleared my throat and said to Zoila in a low, threatening voice, "You coming here is completely unacceptable and over the top, even for you. I'm sorry you're so upset, but I'm married to Jenna now. You have to accept that."

Zoila gazed at us and stood, touching my shoulder. "I'll see you around. I'll love you forever and ever."

She sauntered out of the restaurant, hips swaying, and I leaned in, whispering to Jenna, "I'm terribly sorry about that."

Jenna blew out a breath. "Maybe that's the price we paid for you leaving her. Let's start our evening over. Hello, handsome husband."

Now, I hear footsteps coming down the stairs after Jenna went to get a sweater for Zoila, and my pulse picks up. I tried to escape from Zoila, but she found me and wrapped me in a web of lies I've told.

Zoila and Jenna enter the kitchen and sit at the

counter, side by side. Zoila leans in to my wife and says in a low voice, "He's mine," and I flinch.

Jenna stands and says in a tight voice, "I'll get the appetizers."

She takes a cheese platter from the fridge, adds crackers and sets it down before Zoila. "We thought these crackers might help settle your stomach."

Zoila takes one and chews, wrinkling her nose. She dabs her mouth with a napkin. Pushing the cheese platter away, Zoila makes a face. "No, thanks. I can't stand the taste of garlic and rosemary ever since I started chemo."

My eyebrows shoot up. "Sorry, we didn't know. We had no idea. Sorry about that."

My wife gives me a death glare, but it quickly fades. I say, "How about a slice of cheese, if you don't like the crackers?"

Zoila shakes her head. "I'll pass. I'm eliminating dairy from my diet."

I cock my head, wondering what we're going to eat. The party I suggested is not a party at all. The kitchen is fairly vibrating with an undercurrent of two women sparring without words. I'm exhausted from the whiplash of emotional waves smacking me broadside.

"How about this," I say with false enthusiasm. "We'll eat plain pasta with olive oil and a salad, and I baked a cake for dessert. We can skip the ice cream I picked up at the store."

Jenna beams. "He's sweet, isn't he? He's the best husband ever."

Zoila leans on her elbows. "He's a keeper, all right. Is the pasta gluten-free? I hope so."

I frantically search for the package and read the ingredients. "Yes, thank goodness, I happened to pick up a package and thought we'd try it out. We're safe."

She drums her fingers on the granite counter. "Sure, that sounds good, except for the cake part."

I let out a long sigh. "I wanted to make you a special dinner for your birthday, but I guess I blew it." I look at my wife for support, but she averts her eyes, gazing out the window as our neighbor Jacklyn walks by with her dog.

Clearing my throat, I say, "Do we need to go out for dinner?"

Jenna shakes her head. "No, we're staying in. But hold on, I'll be right back."

Jenna rushes outside to talk to Jacklyn about something, but I can't imagine what would be that important. It's rude to our guest. "I'm sorry," I say to Zoila. "It feels like Jenna's mood is a bit off. But we both want you here, I know we do."

Zoila says, "I thought your idea of eating out was a good one, as long as you're paying for it. After all, it is my birthday."

Jenna marches in the front door followed by our neighbor Jacklyn and her dog Buddy. The three of them pad inside, and Jenna says, "Jacklyn is joining us for dinner. I'll set another place at the table."

My gaze connects with Zoila's, and we both shrug. I say, "Welcome, Jacklyn."

Jacklyn smiles. "Thank you."

Zoila sips sparkling cider and sets the glass down. "I thought because it's my birthday, I get to pick."

Jenna says, "That's only if you're under ten years old, isn't that right, Jacklyn?"

Jacklyn nods. "Absolutely, that only applies to children. Happy birthday, Zoila."

Zoila says in a small voice, "Thanks."

I bite my lip and regret offering to host a birthday dinner. It's taken a wrong turn, and it feels like the worst is yet to come. If this were a spreadsheet at work, I'd delete the file from my computer, but I'm stuck here for the duration. Maybe Jacklyn's presence will provide a pleasant buffer, halting the frigid friction flowing between Jenna and Zoila and bringing the festive birthday dinner back from disaster.

11

JACKLYN

Sitting down at the table, my gaze flits around the table, taking in Jenna's straight-backed posture and Zoila's slouching frail figure. My dog sniffs Zoila and settles down on the floor by me. It seems that Kirk's ghost from the past, Zoila, is haunting him, and Jenna won't release her grip. I'm fine taking in the side show, but I'll be delighted when Buddy and I walk out the door to finish our walk. Being chilled to the bone on a Pacific Northwest winter evening is nothing compared to the storm brewing at this dinner table.

I say to Jenna, "How is work going?"

"Pretty good. I like working from home on marketing plans."

"And you, Zoila, what are you doing for work?" The stilted conversation thus far feels like I'm paddling upstream in a rubber raft. Kirk chews on a fingernail as if it is the main course. Jenna crosses her arms, but Zoila slings her arm over the back of her chair. Buddy is smart enough to doze off and miss the undercurrent of mayhem. He whimpers in his sleep, and I'm tempted to join him.

Zoila studies her glossy fingernails. "I've been doing a little of this and a little of that. I helped Dusty in his office, filling in from time to time, but you ended that arrangement when you took over his business. I've lived in town longer than you knew, before I moved in next door. I've been watching you, Kirk and Jenna."

Jenna and I exchange a quick glance. Kirk looks up from his plate of pasta. The house smells of fish, but there's no seafood on our plates. This is the strangest, most tense dinner I've attended, except for on Christmas Eve, when my son barged in uninvited and took over my party.

Zoila sits on her hands and stares at me. "How is Dusty? I heard you sent him to Shore Lodge. What kind of mother would do that to their son? You strike me as a cruel person, not only to humans, but to poor animals, like innocent raccoons, who can't defend themselves."

I toss my napkin on the table and stare at the thin waif who has red talons for fingernails. How Zoila managed to navigate life this far without someone bopping her in the nose is a miracle. Buddy gets up and shakes, metal tags clanking.

I say, "I'm a mother who takes care of her son, that's who. A mother who realizes her son needs fulltime care with physical therapy and occupational therapy several times a day. Dusty is getting the best care available."

Zoila pouts her full red lips. "Can Dusty talk yet? Because we have unfinished business between us. He made promises he didn't keep."

I shrug. I bet my son made a lot of promises before he went broke and was buried in an avalanche. He honed the art of bullshitting and could win an Olympic medal in it. "No, he's not able to speak yet. He talked big and follow through wasn't his greatest strength. He's more of a take your money and run kind of guy, if you know what I mean."

Zoila sniffs. "If I were his mom, I'd be saying nice things. I wouldn't put him down."

Everything about Zoila rubs me the wrong way, but in an effort to repair neighborly relations, I rest a hand on the back of the chair and say, "How are your cancer treatments going? I can drive you to infusion appointments, if needed."

She shakes her head vigorously, as if the idea of riding in a car with me repels her. "Thanks, but Kirk drives me. I love his jokes. It takes me back to the good old days, where we'd talk and laugh all night."

A flash of concern crosses Jenna's face, and Kirk nods to her. Jenna says, "I'll be driving you to chemo infusions from now on. Kirk has work to do."

Zoila pouts. "Surely, Kirk, you can take a little lunch break to drop me off."

He shakes his head. "Sorry, but work calls."

Zoila twirls a lock of long brown hair around her fingers. "Are you sure?" She tilts her head and batts her eyelashes at Kirk, but he just shrugs. Zoila covers her mouth and giggles. "Come on, Kirk, drive this wife to treatment. I need your help. I wouldn't ask if I didn't mean it."

Jenna's jaw clenches, and she grips the table edge.

Kirk stares at his fork and says, "Ex-wife."

The turns this dinner has taken are too strange for me, and I glance at Jenna, wondering how in the world she can live next door to a woman who is audaciously flirting with her husband. Being in the thick of these shenanigans would drive me batty.

I say, "Thank you for the dinner invitation. Buddy and I have to finish our walk before the rain hits. We're expecting a downpour by midnight."

I say goodbye, hurrying out the door, and buckets of rain burst through the clouds, pouring down and drenching us. I turn up my face as raindrops splash down and breathe a sigh of relief for having escaped from the pressure-cooker in my neighbor's house. The triangle of tension was crackling, ready to burst into flames, and Zoila is the spark to set off an out-of-control fire.

Stepping around puddles on the street, I shake my head at how different we humans can be. Buddy and I march through the wind and rain. I say to him, "No raccoons are out tonight, which is a welcome change. I won't let them attack you again, sweet dog. You're a good boy."

The wind howls, and my rain jacket hood flies back, exposing my head. Rain drops plop down on my scalp, water drips into my eyes, and we hurry home. For all I know, Kirk might be enjoying the attention he's getting from two women who love him. If he isn't, why is he letting Zoila push him around? I'll have to ask Jenna when I see her. What an untenable situation, living close to your husband's former wife. I know I couldn't live with that irritation, drip, drip, dripping, wearing you down.

.

12

KIRK

As I head to the kitchen to get the birthday cake I baked, Jenna joins me, and the stiffness to her spine and cold reserve tells me I've greatly offended her in some way. If she's ticked off about the sweater I offered Zoila, she needs to get over it. Zoila is chilled to the bone, and anyone with a heart would want to help her. Zoila is a thin, fragile shell of the person she once was.

Jenna taps my shoulder, and I flinch. She says in a low voice, "We need to have a serious talk after she leaves tonight."

I wince and wonder what she wants to say. I'm torn between two women, each pulling at me with different purposes. I stick three birthday candles in the cake and take out a lighter, flicking it and concentrating on lighting the yellow and white-striped candles. "Sure, whatever you want."

Jenna leans in. "You need to stand up to her."

"I hear you loud and clear. But now is not the time to discuss it. Let's go out there and join her."

She whispers, "She has you wrapped around her fingers. What's going on?"

"I have my reasons, but I can't discuss them. It's between me and her."

Jenna's mouth falls open. She crosses her arms, and I know I've said the wrong thing. She hisses, "You have secrets with her, and you won't tell me? I'm your wife."

I glance toward the dining room. "Hon, this isn't the time or place. Let's take the cake out and get this dinner over with. I'm sorry I invited her, but we can't be rude. She's sick."

Jenna looks me in the eye, and my hands tremble, holding the cake. My pulse quickens, recalling decisions I've made that I regret. She takes the cake from me and says, "Fine, let's go, but I have things to tell you when we're alone."

My chest tightens, and I follow her into the dining room, where we sing Happy Birthday with gusto. Jenna places the round two-layer cake in front of Zoila, who glances up and goes back to her phone screen.

Gesturing to the cake, I say, "Happy Birthday. How about blowing out the candles?"

Zoila sets her phone down. "I was checking in with my cancer support group, since you two took so long in the kitchen." She blows out the candles, and my eyes fix on her luscious full lips, which survived the disaster chemo has heaped on her frail body. She picks up a candle, chewing on the end, and spits wax into a napkin.

I smile, having witnessed this behavior before, but Jenna wrinkles her nose.

Wiping her mouth, Zoila says to me, "Bet you thought I stopped doing that, didn't you? If you'd like to know what I wished for, it was for peace, harmony and health for the three of us."

Jenna sits and flashes a tight smile. "That's a good wish, and I hope it comes true. Tell us more about how you're feeling. My mom went through cancer treatment, and I know it can be a lot to deal with."

Zoila's cheekbones are sharply defined. She looks close to gaunt. I pat Zoila's hand, and Jenna sits up straight. I say to Zoila, "Yes, tell us how you're feeling. Can I get anything for you? You're looking thin these days."

A slight smile flickers across her face and disappears. "I'd like some of that whiskey you used to drink."

My wife arches an eyebrow. "I thought people on chemo weren't supposed to drink."

Zoila shrugs. "Everyone makes their own choices. I limit my alcohol intake, but this is a special occasion, isn't it? Not every day is my birthday."

The cake sits ignored, and I hurry to the kitchen, putting ice cubes in a heavy base bar glass. Heading back to the dining room, I smile, recalling when Jenna and I bought the set of bar glasses during a weekend trip to Seattle. We stayed at a swanky hotel downtown, and when we came home, I had to do some quick bookkeeping maneuvers at work to cover the cost of our mini-vacation.

Pouring a finger of booze on four ice cubes, I hand the glass to Zoila. No need to be a bad influence on her, when her body is going through so much.

She smiles, tilting her head. "Kirk, come on, this is a baby portion. Give it to me, like you used to. You know exactly what I want, and not just with beverages."

Jenna's jaw drops. My body goes still, and I hold my breath. After a beat, I say, "I don't think you meant that to sound like it did, so I'll ignore it."

Zoila plays with a lock of long brown hair. "I knew what I was saying. You know me the best of anyone I know."

Jenna gets up and stands at the window, looking into the dark night. Her back is to us, and she crosses her arms. A chill hangs over the conversation, and I know I should tell my former wife to leave our home, never to return, but I can't bring myself to confront her for fear she'll tell Jenna what I did. I doubt Jenna would love a man who embezzles, and that's why I haven't told her my secrets.

Picking up Zoila's drink, I add more of the amber

liquid that I was saving for a special occasion with my wife. When I set it down before her, Zoila grabs my arm, latching on, and says, "Thanks, you're the best. We were so good together. It's a shame it ended, isn't it?"

I break into a coughing fit, and Jenna gives me a side look that means we'll have a heavy discussion tonight before going to bed, when all I'll want to do is collapse and forget about my misguided idea to bring the three of us together under one roof to celebrate my former wife's birthday. This is the worst birthday dinner in history, and it's all my fault.

I ask Jenna, "Can I get you a drink?"

She smiles, but it looks forced. "Sure, as long as you're having one. We were saving it for a special occasion, weren't we?"

I pour two drinks and skip the ice cubes, handing one to Jenna while Zoila watches. I choke out a chuckle, but it sounds strained, and raise my glass. "This is a special occasion. Happy Birthday, Zoila."

We sip smoky whiskey, and it burns going down my throat. Jenna and I sit at the table with Zoila, who twirls a strand of hair around her finger. The cake waits for anyone to want a slice, but so far no one cares about dessert. Zoila is clearly in charge, and we're two pawns awaiting her next move.

Zoila takes a sip and sets down her glass, saying in a soft voice, "Actually, there is something you two could do, if you really want to help me out."

Jenna pours more whiskey into her glass and comes back to the table. She usually takes it with two ice cubes, so I know I'm in trouble when she's drinking whiskey neat and onto her second drink.

Jenna raises her eyebrows and glances at me, before turning to Zoila. "What would that be?"

13

JACKLYN

Buddy and I finish our evening walk, plodding through rain and getting soaked. Near home, I glance over at Jenna's house, which she owned before she met Kirk. From what I've heard from Jenna, they had a good marriage. But when Kirk rented the house next door for his ex-wife, he basically taped together two sticks of dynamite and lit a slow fuse. An explosion is bound to occur at some point, and over dinner, it felt like they were building toward a brutal end. I'm not sure if Kirk realizes how bad an idea it was to install Zoila next door to his wonderful new wife.

I say in a low voice to Buddy, "I'm glad we escaped that dinner when we did. I couldn't stay in that house a moment longer."

Buddy barks at a squirrel scampering up a tree.

Marching through the rain, I say, "Good luck to them,

because I doubt Kirk sees how Zoila is manipulating him. But it's not my life, and as Mercury says, I should keep my nose out of it."

I unlock the door to my bungalow, and we tromp inside. My phone rings, and Buddy shakes, sending water droplets flying. I pull out my phone and say, "Hello?"

A woman says in a stern voice, "Is this Jacklyn Stone?"

"Yes."

"This is the nurse on duty at Shore Lodge. We've had an incident with your son."

"Oh, no. What happened?"

"He tried to bite one of our aides."

My mouth hangs open.

She says, "Are you still there?"

"Yes, I just don't know what to say. I'm shocked."

"We are too. We had to administer a sedative. Do we have permission to continue giving medications like that, if needed?"

My mind flashes back to when Nurse Wright jabbed me with a needle to sedate me when I was at Shore Lodge and how I slumped down to the cold, hard floor. Shaking my head, I say, "Do what's best to protect the staff. I don't want them getting hurt. Dusty does have a temper."

"We suspect he's acting out because he isn't able to walk or talk."

I sigh. "He's always been a stewpot simmering on the stove, boiling over when it was least expected. Is he still getting physical therapy and occupational therapy?"

"Yes, we're doing all we can for him to recover his abilities."

"Good."

She says, "We'll have to restrain him if he doesn't calm down. We're keeping a close eye on him."

I press my lips together, recalling Mrs. Skidmore, a resident in Shore Lodge's psych ward, who was restrained much of the time, because otherwise, she'd scratch herself and draw blood or yank her hair out by the roots. "I understand. Do what you must. By the way, how is Mrs. Skidmore? Is she still singing and sounding like a screeching bird?"

The nurse chuckles. "Yes, she is, but if anyone asks, I didn't say that, given patient confidentiality rules."

"She must have really been through the wringer to end up that way."

"I can't comment, but we do have some very sad cases here. Well, I just wanted to let you know about your son's situation. Are you thinking of visiting sometime soon?"

"No, I'm not ready for that yet."

"I understand. I was told he admitted you to our facility and yet you were a grieving widow of sound mind and body? That must have been hard to accept."

I clench my fists. "I'm still stung from his betrayal and haven't gotten over it yet. Thank you for calling and good night."

"Goodbye."

We hang up, and I blow out a breath. In what wild

world would I have foreseen the night I escaped from Shore Lodge that one day I'd admit my own, angry, calculating son to the same facility in the secure ward? Life has brought us back full circle, except Dusty is the one about to be restrained to a chair, not me.

14

———

JENNA

I study Kirk's face, where his left eye twitches with a nervous tic, and recall how when we were first married, he could do no wrong. Tonight, however, he's landed face down in a cow pie, and I'm forced to review my options. From his performance tonight, it's clear he has chosen Zoila over me in every way except for living together. I'm trapped between them, and I want choices.

My pulse picks up, and I ponder the possibilities of how to extricate myself from this tangled mess. I'm confused. Is he still in love with her? This is my house, and I invited him to come live with me when we were married. I suppose if I can't get her to move out of the neighborhood, I could ask him to leave. But that's a final, unfortunate solution for two people who, until Zoila appeared next door, were deeply in love, or so I thought.

I tap a finger to my lips. Every board and window and door is dear to me, because the house was left to me by my father in his will. This was his family's home and where he grew up. He wanted this place to be my refuge from the world, like it was for him until he died peacefully in his sleep. He told me in his last days he wanted me to treasure it like he did and in our family home, I'd always be safe.

Sipping whiskey, I ponder what to do. My muscles tense, and I'm ready for a fight. Trapped by Zoila's machinations, I must do something. Maybe Jacklyn will help me come up with a plan. I'll discuss it with her tomorrow.

"Hon," Kirk says, waving a hand in front of my face. "Everything all right?"

I shrug. "I'm just distracted. Zoila, you were about to say something. You had an idea?"

She tilts her head and smiles at Kirk. "I've changed my mind. I'll wait to bring it up. It's not the right time."

My stomach knots, dreading what is coming next, and the pasta I ate forms a brick in my belly. I glance at my phone for the time and grit my teeth. It is only seven o'clock, even though it feels much later. From the way Kirk and Zoila are dug into their chairs, holding drinks, I might have an hour or more to endure her presence before we say goodnight. But it's her birthday, and she seems lonely, so I'll be polite and won't walk her to the door now. Tomorrow, with a fresh perspective, I'll figure out exactly what to do.

15

IRENA

I shove a key in the door at my former boyfriend's house, but the lock won't open. I jiggle the key until it turns. Kelly follows me inside, and I flick on a light switch, but the house remains dark on a gloomy January evening in the Pacific Northwest.

Kelly says, "It stinks in here."

"It does. I'll have to clean the place. Want to help?"

"Not really. I want to go home and take a nap instead."

I arch an eyebrow, but she can't see my face in the dark. Using our phones, we turn on flashlight apps and enter the kitchen. Dust covers the espresso maker, which Buzz prized. A mug in the sink with coffee shows spots of furry mold.

I wrinkle my nose and wander down a hall. Kelly turns into the living room, but I venture into the main bedroom and inhale what remains of his scent mixed with the smell of dusty old books. Perching on the edge of his bed, I wipe a tear from my cheek. I was angry at him for telling me lies and refused to marry him, but I wish he was still alive. He was the first friend I made when I moved to town.

Kelly calls, "Mom, come here."

I stride down the hall to his second bedroom, which he kept as a home office. Kelly yanks on a closet door, but it doesn't open. "Why is this locked, and the others are open?"

I cock my head. "I don't know. Let's see if one of these keys will open it."

Trying two keys, the second one slides in and turns. I touch the cold metal knob, realizing Buzz might have been the last one to touch this before he departed this earth by jumping off Jackson Bridge. At least that's what we think happened. No one knows, because his body hasn't been found. He might have been carried north by currents, or he could have sunk down to the depths and become fish food.

Kelly says, "I wonder what's in there. Open it, and let's see."

Slowly opening the door, I glance inside and gasp. My grade school picture sits in a silver frame, surrounded by votive candles. A white leather-bound book makes the scene look like a shrine, but I don't dare take a close look in front of my daughter.

Goosebumps prick my flesh, and I shiver. The closet

feels like a secret, creepy, private space, and we're intruders. Closing the door and locking it, I lean back against it.

She frowns. "What's in there? I didn't get a good look."

"It's something I think he meant only for me to see. I'll take a look another time and maybe tell you later. Come on. We've looked enough. Let's go home and eat dinner."

"But I didn't get to see what's in the closet. Why did he leave you the house and the boat and the bookstore, and I only got the Dickens set of books?"

I shrug. "It might be because he loved me. He was the one always looking out for me."

We step outside, and I lock the house. Light rain falls on our hair and faces. We climb in the car, and I slide the key in the ignition, starting it.

Kelly says, "I should've gotten more. He was going to be my step-father, before he attacked my dad and you told him off."

Blowing out a breath, I keep my complicated feelings to myself about the man I loved who carried secrets and harbored a deep, dark hidden rage. He wounded our friend Jack and left him for dead by the wharf. Shaking my head, I say, "Why don't you appreciate what you have, instead of whining about what you didn't get?"

We're silent on the ride home, because I've said the unthinkable and implied she was being selfish. But she has a reason to be unhappy now and complain about every little thing wrong in her life, after she was abducted by my dad and FBI agents brought her home. She did bring many of her problems on herself though, like running around at night with the wrong crowd, wielding a whip.

I unlock our front door and say, "I'll talk to your father tomorrow about the idea of you being home schooled."

She shuffles down the hall, looking at the floor. My cheerful girl has turned into a mercurial, traumatized teenager who is taunted by her peers for being different. I know what that's like, from my childhood, and I intend to sort this out however I can to make her whole again.

16

JACKLYN

Stepping into the kitchen, I give Buddy a scoop of kibble for his second dinner, and he gobbles it down. Wondering what's going on with Jenna's strange situation, I pull out my phone and text her. 'Sorry I had to leave. Hope you survive the drama.'

Jenna texts back. 'Thanks for coming by to break up the tension. We're at level nine on a ten scale. She's leaning on his every word, flirting. Can't get much worse.'

I text her a heart emoji and don't hear back. I hope they're enjoying a game of gin rummy, crazy eights, or a board game to distract themselves from odd, uncomfortable dynamics, where past and present loves clash.

Mercury's words about not interfering run through my mind, ringing a warning bell, but I shrug off his caution and text Jenna. 'Does Kirk know how awful this situation is making you feel? He needs to hear it from you. Tell him.'

There's dead silence for a few minutes and then my phone dings with a message. 'This is Kirk. I don't appreciate you butting in. This is a private matter, so stay out of it. Zoila is sick and needs our support.'

My face heats, and I run my hands over my cheeks. I should have put my feet up and read a book instead of stirring up trouble by texting. I let out a groan, and my dog sits, staring at me.

I release a sigh. "It seems I've become the neighborhood busy body, poking my nose where it doesn't belong. I hope I didn't put a rift between Jenna and her husband."

I fill a mug with water and carry it to the living, setting it on a side table and plopping down on the couch. Buddy hops up next to me, and I pat his soft fur, saying, "I'll keep my trap shut more often from now on."

I sit and ruminate about what a wild winter it has been, from a boat trip to Shore Lodge to rescue my friends, a Christmas Eve dinner party during a storm, to my son getting buried in an avalanche. Now we have a tangled mess down the block, because Kirk moved his ex-wife next door to his wife, and they're flinging barbs, fighting over him.

Wind howls, battering the house, and window panes rattle. The house shudders, but I sit back and stare at an ash-filled empty fireplace, pondering how I might honor the one-year anniversary of my husband's passing.

I nod to myself. I'll plant a tree in the yard and scatter Albert's ashes in the soil. Dusty won't be there, because he's on Cedar Island in a locked ward, but I'll invite my daughter Rose and my grandson.

With a frown, my mind drifts back to when Dusty broke into my house, bringing another man and staging a home invasion. I just about died of fright that night. Now, I pick up my library book in my peaceful, quiet home and say to Buddy, who is curled up beside me, "You saved me that night. Good job, you sweet dog."

His brown eyes open, and he blinks before going back to sleep. Pursing my lips, a thought flits past. It's nearing time for me to make a decision about my construction project on a hill above town. Will I proceed with my plan, or put a permanent pause on the project? The environmental survey is due any day, and the cost of paying for four new fire hydrants, plus replacing the water line to adjoining homes, burned up my carefully constructed budget. I might as well have a new hobby of lighting one-hundred-dollar bills on fire.

Buddy twitches in his sleep. I'll deal with the decision of what to do with Stone Estates when I have the environmental survey results in hand. At least I solved the puzzle of what to do with Albert's ashes. One step at a time.

17

JENNA

Zoila shivers and says, "Kirk, would you light a fire for me? I'm so cold." He jumps up and lights the fire I built last week, when I had visions of the two of us enjoying a relaxing evening by a roaring fire. But he's been too busy helping Zoila to hang out with me.

She sits in my favorite leather armchair with her feet up, sipping our special expensive whiskey and laughing loudly at Kirk's jokes. Her slender fingers dance in the air, and she locks eyes with him, giggling like a high school girl. I swallow my seething jealousy and tell myself to calm down. If she truly has cancer, her treatments will come to an end. No need to get overly riled up about this.

Kirk tells a story I've heard many times, and I sit off to the side. I'm the odd one outside of the close-knit twosome seated in front of the fire. Shaking my head at how I'm the one who doesn't belong, even though this is my home, I tell myself to stop being sensitive and join the lively banter peppered with inside jokes. Except I can't. I have no idea who or what they're talking about, dredged up from years ago.

I massage my temples, where a headache throbs, and squirm in the straight back wooden chair. The log in the fireplace is burning down, so surely this evening will end soon. If it doesn't, I'll march her out the door, slam it shut in her face and lock her out of our lives forever.

Zoila says to Kirk, "Will you add a log to the fire? It's not as warm as I'd like it."

I wave my hands. "No need to do that. Let's call it a night."

But Kirk leaps to his feet and carefully places another log on the fire. Grinning at Zoila, he says, "How's that? Better?"

"Yes, thanks." She pulls out her phone and says to Kirk, "I'm doing a livestream, want to be in it?"

He shrugs. "Sure, why not? If it'll make you happy, I'm all for it."

I clench my teeth, counting the minutes until the party that's not a party finally comes to a halt. Letting out a yawn, I'm ready to send her out the front door into the wind and rain, but she scoots close to Kirk, puts an arm around him and faces the camera, holding out her phone.

He leans into her, smiling, and my heart stills. Ice flows through my veins. How did I come to be the person on the sidelines? That should be her role, not mine. She should have gone home long ago, leaving Kirk and I laughing at our own jokes and cleaning up the kitchen together.

Her cheeks are flushed, and she says into the camera, "Here we are, at a birthday get together for guess who? Me! My best friend and former husband, Kirk, invited me over to celebrate. Thanks, Kirk."

She makes a big deal of kissing his cheek, leaving a red lipstick mark, and he smiles. I get up and move my chair away, so I won't be seen frowning and folding my arms, looking ready to fight her off with a pitchfork and chase her out of my home. She's crafty and clever, more than I realized until this moment. She has an armamentarium up her sleeve, with endless ways to entrance my husband. Compared to her flash and sizzle, he must think I'm dull and drab.

Zoila motions to me. "Jenna, come over and Join us. People will love you. You've got a great put together look, enough so you attracted Kirk while he and I were still married, isn't that right? You lured him, and I'm the one who lost everything. I was left penniless with a broken heart." She pouts with her full ruby lips.

I stand and go over to them, popping into the video for a second, just to make a point, but she wraps an angry arm around my neck, choking me and pulling me close. I smell whiskey and garlic on her breath.

I wave at the camera. "I just want to be clear that

nothing happened until these two were divorced. There was no hanky-panky going on."

A flood of comments from nay sayers on Zoila's phone catch my attention.

'Life's losers steal lovers,' says one person.

'Who says hanky-panky? What does that even mean?'

'Go, Zoila! Out the cheaters and expose them. They look guilty to me.'

My stomach roils, and I tap Kirk on the arm. He looks over, smiling and not in touch with what is happening. I hiss in his ear, "This little drama could ruin our careers. Stop this, right now."

He waves it off. "She means well. It's just a bit of fun."

Steam might as well be blowing out of my ears. I stand behind Zoila, watch comments roll in and grind my teeth.

One person writes, 'Where do those losers who hurt Zoila work? Let's send in complaints."

'We'll bury their bosses with the truth & they'll get fired.'

'Justice for Zoila, the warrior!'

I rest a hand on my acidic stomach.

Another writes, 'Where do they live? Let's trash their house.'

'Throw rocks through their windows tonight.'

I stride over to Kirk, who is not reading the comments. He pats Zoila's shoulder. "Go on, tell them how amazing you are at surviving chemo treatments. You're going to beat cancer. If anyone can, you will. You deserve it."

I press my lips together and glower at him. He's pandering to her, but with a subtle undertone of fear evidenced in his squirming body language. Something odd is going on between my husband and his ex-wife, and the dynamics are way off and out of balance. She seems to hold the power in the relationship.

I swallow and release my past regrets. I didn't know Kirk was married when I met him, and he told me on our first date that he'd been separated from this wife for a year. He told me he had filed for divorce, but that wasn't true. That should have been my first clue, blinking bright as a neon sign early in dating, but I believed the lies he told. Only later did it come out that he was dating me and married to Zoila at the same time, which I never would have allowed, had I known. When we married, we moved to this small town into the house I inherited from my father and used on weekends. I naively assumed she'd never find us, holding onto wishful thinking and hopes, and yet here we are, caught in the camera's glare and in her grip, guilty as charged.

I give up on Kirk gaining common sense and go over to the window, pacing and wanting this evening to end. I'm trapped in my home with a guest I never wanted to host. I've got to do something to fix this. My fingers itch to get on my computer and research my options, but I stay in the room to monitor the incendiary situation. I must see what she'll do next and how my husband will act.

Clenching my jaw, I'm teetering between retaining an

ounce of love for him, or wishing he'd drive off a ferry dock and sink to the bottom of the Salish Sea. It'll be too late for poor Kirk, and we'll mourn him, giving him a quiet send-off he deserves, as an unabashed flirt and a man who is oblivious to his wife's seething rage.

Zoila flashes Kirk a wide smile and turns to the camera. "Now you can see why I love this man so much. He's a keeper. Isn't that right, Jenna?"

I plaster a smile on my face. "Absolutely. He's the best." I lean over and whisper in Kirk's ear, "We've got to stop this madness. Shut it down and send her home. If you don't, I will."

He doesn't look my way, apparently dazzled by Zoila's ease on camera with her followers. He swats away my concern, waving a hand in the air, and whispers, "Don't worry about it. Just relax."

I furrow my brow and bite my lower lip.

Zoila speaks into the camera, "One day, when my hair was falling out from cancer treatments, I looked in the mirror and I thought, I can survive this and live to tell the story to inspire others. And you out there, you can get through any challenges in your path, just like I'm doing. And that's why I gathered all of you together on my birthday tonight, because I've got a very special announcement."

I cross my arms, wondering what she's about to say. Is she moving back to the city? I hope so. With a slight smile,

I imagine Zoila driving away and leaving Millersville for good.

She holds up her phone, so our faces appear on the screen, and I step out of the frame, tapping a toe and glancing at the door, hoping she'll soon make her exit.

She says, "So, what's my big news? Drum roll, please. Kirk, use your band skills from high school."

Kirk obliges and drums on the arm of his chair, grinning at the camera. I die a little bit inside, watching him fall into her siren's snare.

"This is my birthday, and I'm proud and blessed to have made it one more year on this planet. I'm lucky to have followers like you, and knowing each and every one of you is what keeps me going when I can't get out of bed. Thank you for your love and encouragement and supportive comments. My announcement is, I'm pleased to say these two wonderful, fine people have offered to take me into their home until I get better. We'll live together under one roof, and they'll be my support team. Isn't that great?"

My jaw drops, and my pulse picks up. I can't have heard right. She's made it up on the spot, I suspect, for social media engagement and likes, and perhaps most importantly, to hold my husband's attention and have him under her thumb for every minute of every hour of every day for as long as she wants to play her games.

Kirk smiles and tilts his head, as if hearing what she said on a delayed relay.

I stride over to her and grab the phone, ripping it out of her hands. I turn it off and slip it into my pocket. Putting my hands on my hips, I say to the two people who are way too cozy, sitting side by side and staring at me as if I'm the enemy, "Zoila, you are not moving into my house. Get out right now. This party is over. Goodbye."

Glass shatters, and a brick flies through the window, landing on the floor with a thud. They jump to their feet, and Zoila screams, running into Kirk's open arms. She sobs. "I'm scared."

"There, there," he says. "I'm sorry she upset you. We'll talk it over, and she'll come around. And she'll give you your phone back, won't she?"

My hands turn cold. "She riled up people online enough, so they're throwing bricks through our window. Can't you see that?"

They look at each other, and Kirk shrugs. "What about her phone?"

I say, "She can have the phone when she leaves. No more videos, and Zoila, you're not moving in with us."

My husband cocks his head. "It was going to be a surprise."

I put my hands on my hips. "Yeah, you surprised me all right. Are you saying this is okay with you?"

Kirk keeps his arm around her, as if it is the most natural thing in the world to do. He stares at the floor and says, "Yes."

Marching up to him, I stick a finger in his face. "She

will not live under my roof. You two are fawning all over each other, and I'm sick of it. Zoila, get out right now."

Kirk cocks his head. "Zoila and I made the decision while you were in the bathroom. I was going to tell you later, so you'd have time to absorb it. But this is a great idea. We'll live together and support Zoila on her healing journey. It'll work, and you just need to keep an open mind. Don't be so negative. You've changed so much in the last few months."

Cold wind blows through the broken window pane, rushing into the house. I say, "It's a crazy idea. This is my house, and she's not moving in. She put our safety at risk with her video, and a brick flew through the window, but you're acting like it's no big deal. Whose side are you on?"

They stand side by side, watching me, as if I'm out of line. Zoila doesn't move away from Kirk, and he doesn't come over to me. A silence settles over the room.

Pointing at Zoila, who leans against Kirk, I say, "What do you have over him?"

She shrugs and smiles. Kirk stares at glass shards and the brick on the wood floor.

I tap a finger to my lips. "So, that's what's going on. You two have a secret, and Zoila, you're using it against him."

Her smile widens, but he frowns, not meeting my gaze.

I clear my throat. "Whatever it is, I don't need to know. I'm done with both of you. Get out. Go next door and get out of my sight."

My stomach churns, and I run to the bathroom,

locking the door and leaning over the toilet, retching and losing the little dinner I ate. I flush the toilet, letting the toilet lid fall with a clang, and turn on the tap, washing my hands and wiping my mouth. No way will I put up with their cozy act. They had better be gone.

Wiping my wet hands on a towel, I open the door. But there they are, Zoila and Kirk, standing in the hall facing me when I emerge from the bathroom.

Zoila comes over and opens her hands. "Everything okay?"

I snort. "No, it is definitely not okay. Do me a favor and go home. Take Kirk with you."

18

DUSTY

I grit my teeth and glare, sitting parked in a wheelchair in the hall. I'll never accept living at Shore Lodge, with its white walls, bright lights and underlying urine odors masked by lemon-scented cleaning products. I want to live in my cabin by the mountains and go hiking. I want to talk. Concentrating hard, I try to wiggle my fingers.

An aide in white walks by, and she stops. "Look, he's moving his hands."

Nurse Wright glances at me. "There's hope for him yet."

I cough, hawking up phlegm, and an aide with brown eyes looks away. I'm a parasite and a pariah. I want to get out of here and do things I've never done before. I'll work hard to get to where I'll be seeing this stark institution in my rear-view mirror.

This is my mother's fault. If not for her, I would've stayed in Millersville and never ventured into the mountains. She goaded me into going into the snow. She put me here in this horrible hellhole. I'll make it my mission to get better, return to town and make her regret her decision to lock me in Shore Lodge.

19

KIRK

Jenna runs into the bathroom, slamming the door, and I start to follow her, but Zoila tugs on my arm and holds me back. She says, "Wait, let her be and give her a moment to herself. I really appreciate your support in all of this."

I jerk my hand away, which is what I should have done before, but she comes close, giving me a hug. I inhale her scent and vaguely smell vanilla and fresh baked snickerdoodle cookies, bringing me back to when we were first married. We baked cookies together in our little apartment on weekends. But that was before I knew who she is below the surface, a plotting, cunning woman who feels fine taking what isn't hers.

I step back from Zoila, shaking my head. If I'm not careful, she'll drain me dry financially and ruin my marriage to Jenna. The toilet flushes, and I glance at the bathroom door, realizing my relationship with Jenna may be over. I can't play both sides and flirt with my ex-wife in front of Jenna. Chalk it up to yet another mistake I've made.

I swallow hard and vow to make amends with Jenna. Being in Zoila's clutches would put me in a dark place, with no way out except down. I'd be back to doing her bidding and stealing money from employers.

Zoila looks me in the eye. "I want to thank you for supporting me during this difficult time. I couldn't do this without you. Your help means so much to me."

My throat is dry, and I cough. "We made a mistake, announcing it like that. And you put our home in danger with your video. We'd better slow down, for Jenna's sake."

Zoila whispers to me as the bathroom door slowly opens. "After we see how she is, I'll go upstairs to check out where I'll sleep. I'll start by staying over tonight."

Ignoring Zoila, I walk toward my frowning wife and open my arms. "Hey, hon, I'm sorry about that. It was all a misunderstanding. Let me make it up to you."

She scowls, which is not a good look on her. Her jaw tenses, and she stops two feet away, crossing her arms. She says, "The way you're acting isn't right, and I won't put up with it. Don't invite her into our home ever again."

I wince, because I know she's right, but I'm powerless to push Zoila away. If I do, she'll expose me, and I'll end up in jail. "Let me explain, so you'll understand."

Zoila says, "I'll just take a look upstairs and let you two

talk." She climbs the steps at a rapid rate, faster than I thought she could manage, given how weak she is from cancer treatment.

Jenna glares at me. "No amount of explaining will dig you out of this hole you dug for yourself. I can't believe you're acting like it's normal. You're threatening our marriage and it's about to shatter, like the glass on the floor. Do you realize this?"

Cold air blows through a gaping hole in the window. I hold up my hands. "We can't turn her away when she needs our help. She has no one else to turn to. We have no choice."

Jenna frowns. "Maybe that's because she repels people. Maybe that's her fault, and she needs to deal with it."

I tilt my head. "Hon, what's going on? You're normally kind and considerate and fun to be around, but I haven't seen that side of you tonight. Where's your sense of compassion?"

She huffs out a breath and glances upstairs. Floorboards overhead creak, and I get the feeling this is hopeless. I can't hold onto two women at once. I must pick between a future laden with secrets and lies, supporting Zoila, or step into the light with Jenna. But if I stay with Jenna, Zoila will take our money, ruin my marriage by flirting with me and expose my crimes. Do I want to be a free man or locked in jail?

Jenna eyes me. "My compassion flew out the window

when you acted like you were in love with her in the video, holding her. I'm fed up. This is the bright line in the sand for me. If you don't change, I'm out."

I put my hands together. "Please don't do that. I'll try. It was just a video, and I was having fun. What harm can a video do?"

Jenna says, "It breaks windows."

20

ZOILA

I'm in the guest bedroom next to the master when Jenna charges upstairs. I open the closet to see if there's enough room for my clothes. While I'm living here, I'll prance around in flimsy negligees to put a rift in their marriage.

Jenna stops in the doorway, planting her feet apart. "You won't be living here, so you can stop sneaking around, looking in rooms."

I shrug. "This room is just fine for my needs."

She shakes her head. "You're not moving in."

I lean against a white wall. "Kirk said I could pick which ever bedroom I wanted. And I like this one."

Her eyes open wide. "He told you to pick one?"

I nod. "That's right. I guess we know who is more important, now that I'm sick. You wouldn't understand what it's like, being healthy. I can barely get out of bed most mornings and drag myself to treatment. I'm exhausted. I can't even cook for myself. This room is a perfect place for me to stay until I recover."

I gesture to the spacious room with a large window facing the back garden. I want to get under her skin, so she'll leave him. I want them to hurt as much as they hurt me.

She rests a hand on her hip. 'Exactly what kind of cancer do you have?"

"That's private information, and I don't want to share it with you, not with your negative attitude toward me."

Her eyes narrow. "I think you're making it up to get attention and more views online. I'm right, aren't I? You're not sick."

She fixes her gaze on me, and I put a hand to my chest. "I'm disappointed you'd think that. That's cold and callous to question my diagnosis by a doctor. With you being Kirk's wife, I expected more from you, because he's open-hearted and supportive on my cancer journey. I'm truly ill and shouldn't have to defend myself. Shame on you for questioning it."

She taps a toe.

I point to the closet and change the subject. "The closet space in this room works for me, and I'll stay until I get better, in a year or two. Kirk said I was welcome to stay as long as I liked."

Jenna coughs. In a tight voice, she says, "Over my dead body."

"I'm the one who might die. You don't understand how difficult this is, but Kirk does. That's why he suggested I move in."

She stomps off, but I poke my head into the hall and say, "Want to help me move my stuff? It's heavy, and I could use a hand. I'd like to clear out of the house next door tonight, so the owners can come back, and Kirk won't have to pay rent there anymore."

She flinches and stares. "Are you saying Kirk is paying your rent?"

"Why sure, that's what he offered to do. It was very gentlemanly, don't you think? I can't work in this condition. I need to take two long naps a day."

Jenna points a trembling finger at me. "You are a manipulator."

I smile. "Why, yes, thanks, I guess I am."

"You're controlling him, and he doesn't know it."

"You might as well admit that I've won. He's all mine except in marriage, and he'll do anything I say."

Kirk comes up the steps. "What's all the fuss? I heard you downstairs. Can't we all get along and come together to support Zoila?"

"Good idea," I say, staring at his wife.

She turns and goes into the master bedroom, locking the door. I hear the water running for a bath. I hurry into the other bathroom upstairs and open the spigot, filling a tub, so she'll struggle to get enough hot water and won't be able to enjoy herself.

Slipping into hot water in the tub, I sigh and my muscles relax. My snare was set, the trap was sprung, and my plans are coming to fruition. A broad smile spreads across my face. Slowly but surely, my plan is coming together.

Down the hall, I hear Jenna say in a loud voice, "The hot water ran out, and I can't take a bath. She used it all."

Kirk says, "She'll only be here a short while. It won't be forever. Let it go."

I smile and slip deeper into hot water. Little does he know I plan to stay here for a very long time. In fact, I might never leave. By the time I'm in remission, I predict Jenna will have up and left him, which is what I want.

21

JACKLYN

I text my daughter Rose about my plan. 'I'm going to plant a tree and bury your father's ashes with it. Would you like to be here when that happens?' While I wait for her reply, I get off the sofa and go in the kitchen, brewing a cup of tea. It's too late to imbibe in my favorite beverage, strong black coffee. Wind howls and tree branches sway, dancing in the wind, but my dog and I are snug inside. This is not a night to be out roaming in the dark, and it is also not a good time to be residing in Jenna's house, where tension was served as a main course for dinner.

I pour hot water into a mug, add a peppermint tea bag and take it to the living room, where Buddy is curled up on the couch. I set the mug down on a side table, and my phone dings with a message.

Rose texts, 'Yes, I want to be there when you do it. I'll bring Max. Weekends work best. Let me know when.'

'This Saturday at noon?'

'That's great. See you then.'

Holding a steaming mug under my nose, I inhale the soothing scent of mint and make a mental note to buy a tree and potting soil and have my shovel ready, along with a few words, for the Saturday event. I've been dithering about what to do with Albert's ashes, and I hope this will give me closure. I'd like to put it in the past, if that's possible.

Resting a hand on my chest, I ruminate about how grief sticks with us, even if we pretend otherwise. After Albert died, I discovered he withheld important medical and financial information and, in a way, I fell into a hole he dug, right in my own front yard. I never thought to double check what he said. I trusted him implicitly, which is not what I'd recommend my neighbor Jenna do. Things have taken a nasty turn in that house, and I wish her luck.

I shrug. Life is like a river, Albert used to say, that twists and turns, and where it goes, no one knows. We're just along for the ride.

I check my email and see one from the company conducting an environmental survey for my housing development on a hill above town. Taking a sip of tea, I read the email and almost drop the mug on the rug. There's an eagle's nest in the middle of the proposed building site. "What?"

Buddy looks up, watching me. I set the cup down and pat his back, saying, "Don't worry. I'm just upset because the project is not going how I expected. It's a royal pain in the butt."

He puts his head down and sighs. Musing aloud, I say, "Maybe I should give up on it. Costs are going up, the building site shrank because of the birds, and this is becoming a big, fat hassle. Who knows what will crop up next week and the week after that?"

I pocket my phone and put my feet up on the coffee table. Sipping tea, I consider the idea of getting up and making a French 75 with gin, lemon juice, simple syrup and champagne, but I shelve the idea. A cup of tea, a warm dog and a book is all I need before bed.

Thoughts about the housing development hammer away at the back of my mind, and I frown, mentally swatting them away. If I fixate on my problems, I'll be up worrying all night. I'll tackle the topic of what to do regarding Stone Estates tomorrow. I open my book and am quickly swept away into another world, where the heroine runs a boat rescue business.

22

IRENA

Kelly comes out of her room when I'm folding laundry on the living room couch. She flops down on a chair and says, "I don't know why you wouldn't let me look in the locked closet. I should be able to see anything I want in Buzz's house."

I shrug. "Some things are private, and I'm not sure what he kept in there. It's between him and me."

"Fine, who cares, anyway. I want to be homeschooled here or go to Grand Island. Moving to the island would fix most of my problems, and I wouldn't have to see kids from school except when I come back to town."

I shake my head. "Sorry, but I'm not a fan of the idea, and I need to talk to your dad before any decisions are made. His memory is just coming back, so I don't think he'd want you to leave town. He wants to see you. Plus, homeschooling calls for a lot of responsibility and doing work on your own."

"I can handle it. Just give me a chance. If Dad says I can do either one, are you okay with it?"

Tapping a finger to my lips, I say, "Let me think about it."

She groans, rolling her eyes. "Please, I'm desperate. You can't make me go to school here. I won't do it. I can't."

I change the subject. "How is it going with Plum?"

She rubs her forehead. "Awful. She'll never forgive me."

"You never know, a lot of things can be overlooked and forgiven if the person is big hearted enough. She might come around."

I make a face, realizing I'm not that kind of big-hearted person, because I wouldn't marry Buzz after he fed me lies about what happened to Jack. It turned out Buzz hurt Jack and didn't call for help. I learned he left him with a traumatic brain injury, which was unforgiveable.

I gather folded clothes in my arms and turn toward the hall leading to the bedrooms.

Kelly says, "What's going on? You got quiet all of a sudden."

I stop in my tracks. "I was just thinking about Buzz, and how he hurt your dad and lied about it."

A tear trickles down her cheek. "Yeah, that was bad."

"I'd say that's the kind of thing you can't overlook, that gets between you and the other person, probably forever."

She nods, looking down. "I get that."

Blinking back tears, I say in a tight voice, "But even with all that, I miss Buzz."

She hops up and gives me a hug, and folded clothes fall to the floor, but I don't care. She buries her face in my chest and says in a muffled voice, "I miss him too."

I hold her tight, grateful to have my daughter in my arms. For this moment on a dark winter night, she's the innocent child I knew before my dad took her.

"I love you, Kelly."

"Love you too, Mom."

23

TEX

I'm on a conference call, working from home on Grand Island, when a text comes through on my phone. Kelly, Irena's delightful teenage daughter, writes, 'I know this is a big question, but could I come live with you for a while? I'd do my homework and clean the dishes and go to the schoolhouse on the island.'

I ignore my conference call and text back. 'I've love to have you, but you'll have to get your parents' permission and agree to follow my rules. Tell your mother to call me later tonight.'

'K. Thanks.'

I return to work, but find myself gazing out the wide front window, watching tall grass sway in the wind and beyond that, white caps frothing on two-foot waves. I missed the chance to have my own children, by working so many hours in my younger days, but now that I'm older and wiser, maybe I can make a difference in a thirteen-year-old's life and help steer her in the right direction.

A sailboat plies the channel, and I smile. It will be a huge challenge to have Kelly live under my roof, but I'm up for it. This is the right time to try something like this.

I knock on the wood table for luck and hope I have the patience required to live with a teenager who has been harassed by her peers. She's a damaged bird, but not beyond repair, waiting for a firm, loving person like me to step in and help.

A woman says, "Tex, are you there?"

I smile. "Yes, sorry about that. I was distracted by a possible new development in my life. I'll tell you about it later, if plans come to fruition. Now back to business, how are next quarter's profits looking? Do you expect them to meet market expectations?"

24

JACK

Irena texts me, 'Have time to talk?' I answer back, 'Yes. Call me.' I don't remember being married to her, given my amnesia, but I get the feeling she might have been difficult to live with. She's driven and restless, and I'm surprised I was drawn to that type of person, but maybe the saying is true that opposites attract. In comparison, Abby is sweet, kind and gentle. She's a good person, deep down in her soul.

Irena calls, and I pick up right away. I'm working on getting stronger, after my best friend Buzz hit me, leaving me with a head injury by a wharf. My stomach knots these days at the smell of salt air, but Abby tells me I used to love walking by the water.

Taking a deep breath, I bring myself back to the present and prepare for the whirlwind of energy that Irena brings. "Hello?"

"Hey, we need to talk about Kelly. Is now a good time?"

"Sure, how is she doing?"

"She's really down. Her friend Plum won't talk to her, and kids at school are gossiping about her and making up lies."

I frown. "It's not her fault your dad took her, so they shouldn't do that. They should admire her strength and not be mean."

"We know that, but the little jerks in school don't."

I whoosh out a breath. "We're just lucky she's tough and made it home to us."

Abby wakes up from a nap. "Is that Irena? Put her on speaker. I want to listen."

I tell Irena, "Abby's here too. I'll put you on speaker."

"Hi Abby," Irena says. "How are you feeling? Do you need anything?"

Abby groans. "I need a new body. Can you get that for me? And some vanilla ice cream?"

We chuckle, and Irena says, "I'll bring some over the next time we stop by. And I wish I could give you a new body."

"I want one too," I say. My hand trembles as I hold the phone, so I set it down.

Irena says, "Jack, how are you? Is your memory coming back?"

I shrug and smile at Abby, sitting in a recliner in the house we bought after I got out of the hospital. "I'm happy

I'm alive and getting stronger every day, but my memory has major gaps. Abby fills me in on what I've forgotten."

Irena says, "I'm sorry to bring this up, but do you have a game plan about when you might go back to work and start paying me the overdue child support?"

I cough. "Not yet. I need to get stronger and be able to walk better. Plus I need to help Abby until she recovers."

After a beat of silence, Irena says, "What are you thinking of doing for work? Bartending, like you used to?"

"No, I don't think standing for all those hours would be good for my back. I want to help people who are sick, like I was. I just need to figure out what I want to do. Maybe I'll be an ultrasound or X-ray technician."

Abby jumps in. "We need to give him time. I don't want him to fall down and get hurt again, or get sick and go in the hospital."

Irena sighs. "Understood, but I'll bring this up again in a few months. I need the money to support Kelly and pay for her therapy and other expenses. That's why I'm calling, because Kelly is begging me to be homeschooled, but I'm not home all the time, so that wouldn't be right."

I say, "No, that wouldn't work. And I don't think, in the state we're in, that we could have her live here and be homeschooled, sadly. I'd like to, but we can't at this time."

Abby says, "I agree. I'd love to do that, but we can't right now."

Irena says, "I figured you'd say that. What she really

wants and keeps asking about is to move to Grand Island and live with Tex and go to the schoolhouse on the island, where kids of all ages sit in a room. Tex said there's one teacher for the group."

I cock my head. "She wants to do that? She'd move away from us?"

"Yep, that's what she said. She wants to get out of town for a fresh start. Kids are too mean to her here. She's brought this up several times."

Abby says, "What does Tex say about this idea?"

"Kelly texted her to ask, because I put it off, and Tex said it was fine, but she has rules and Kelly will have to come see us once a week."

"Well, yeah," I say, "of course."

We're silent for a beat, taking it in, and Abby says, "I don't like it, because I want her close. But it might be what's best for her, if she's serious about making a fresh start."

I clear my throat. "Won't she be bored there? There won't be dance lessons or places to shop, just hikes to take and lots of water surrounding an island far from town."

"She says she'll be fine with it," Irena says in a tight voice. "I'm hesitant, but I feel like we should let her try it. If it doesn't work, it was her choice, and she can always come back and enroll in school here."

I nod. "But it's a huge responsibility for Tex to take on. Are you sure she's okay with this? I trust her, but she might be in over her head, overseeing a teenage girl."

Irena says, "I thought of that too, but I suppose we might as well try it. Kelly is desperate and keeps asking me about it. She even mentioned we could move to Montana, but then we'd be far from you and the water, where I make my living. I like living in the same town as you guys."

Abby says, "Us too. And you're a really good Mom to our sweet girl. It's better if we live within a few miles of each other."

I break out coughing, clearing my lungs. "I just thought of something. Are there any trouble makers on the island who might influence Kelly in a negative way? From what Abby says, the three of us got into loads of trouble when we were Kelly's age."

"I'll ask Tex about that," Irena says. "I'll meet the teacher and maybe some parents, if I see them. But kids like that are everywhere. Kelly isn't enclosed in a bubble in town, and she won't be, no matter where she lives."

I glance over at Abby, and we nod to each other. I say, "We agree it's okay to go ahead and try it out. But if it doesn't work, we'll need to come up with another solution."

Irena says, "I'm at a dead-end with ideas, trying to help her. This is the best option, so I'm glad we're in agreement."

I sigh. "Maybe I'm glad I can't remember being thirteen, with all the angst."

Abby says with a smile, "Yeah, you're lucky about that."

"Okay, just to recap," Irena says, "we've got a weird situation on our hands, and we need to fix it for Kelly, if we can. We're okay with her trying out living on Grand Island with Tex, and she'll go to school there. Let's make it on a trial basis for a month and re-evaluate. This is either brave or stupid, but we've got to try."

I swallow. "That's right. And when you take her over to the island, I'm sorry but we're not in good enough shape yet to go on your boat and drop her off. Can you handle that by yourself?" Abby nods to me.

"Yep, I've been doing things by myself for a pretty long time," Irena says, "and I can handle it. I'll tell her to call you when she's settled, but there are parts of the island that don't get cell reception. She might have to stand on the end of the dock facing north to call you on her cell. I hope she won't drop it in the drink."

I groan. "I can just see that happening."

Abby says, "Thanks for calling and asking for our opinion."

"Thanks, guys, love you. Here we go, trying to do our best for our girl."

She hangs up, and I say to Abby, "This parenting business is tough, isn't it? I had no idea."

Abby raises her eyebrows. "You were fairly self-focused and not as concerned about Kelly before your head injury. But now you're a number one Dad. What are we having for dinner? Pizza?"

I grin. "No, I thought I'd serve you cold gruel with anchovies."

She rolls her eyes. "No thanks to that. You joker, you, come here and give me a kiss."

25

IRENA

I email Tex to check in with her and make plans, asking her to call me.

Tex calls five minutes later, and I close my bedroom door, sitting on the bed and speaking in a low voice, so Kelly won't hear. Tex says, "I'm fine with this. Don't be nervous. I had brothers and sisters growing up."

I cringe and study the ceiling. "But this is different. We have a traumatized thirteen-year-old girl who has gone through a lot. Her dad forgot who she was due to his head injury, Buzz died, and my dad kidnapped her. He was taking her to a river, where they'd live in an abandoned fishing shack, and no one would know where she was. She's rattled to her core, and she might not be easy on you."

"You don't need to explain it to me. My best friend growing up went through a heck of a lot. I think I can handle Kelly, but if it turns out I can't, I'll call you and she'll be on a boat ride back to town in a flash."

My chest tightens. "This is a big step. We've never been apart more than a school day. She's used to being around me."

In a reassuring voice, Tex says, "We'll give it a try. It's not like we're committing to something that will last forever. Plus, you'll need to come over here anyway to meet with me and review your progress reports, so you'll see her often enough."

I put a hand to my forehead and moan. "I forgot about the progress reports. With all that's going on, let's skip them this month and the next one and put it off until next year.

She laughs. "You're not weaseling out of best practices on my watch. You'll come over, and we'll review the books. It'll be good for you and help your business grow."

"Fine. When can we come over, so Kelly can start school there? I'd like to talk with the teacher."

"Of course. I already mentioned to her that Kelly might join us when I saw her at the store."

I chuckle. "A store that has not many items but is a great place to gossip?"

"That's the one. Kelly can start in class right away."

"Good, but this is temporary. If she acts out or things are uncomfortable for you in any way, call me. I'm just a boat ride away."

"Agreed. That's the deal."

"And I'll pay for her food while she's there. I don't want to mooch off you."

"Nonsense. One young girl isn't going to break the bank. I need to eat anyway, so what's one more plate?"

"Thank you. We'll revisit that if we need to. Oh, and Jack asked if there were any bad influence kind of kids over there that might make Kelly go astray, if you know what I mean?"

"As you know, kids like that are everywhere, and you can't escape them. I'll bet that we have fewer trouble makers on the island than in town."

I nod. "You might be right. Okay, let's do this. When does it work for us to come over?"

"Tomorrow early afternoon. Let me know when you're on your way."

My eyebrows shoot up. "That soon? I was thinking of next week or the week after."

"Let her fly on her own and try a new environment. I'll watch over her. Don't worry."

I gulp. "We'll see you tomorrow. And thanks, I really appreciate this."

"No problem."

I hang up, and the bedroom door swings open. Kelly shifts her weight from side to side. "Did she say yes? Did Dad and Abby agree? Am I going?"

I jump to my feet and wrap her in a warm hug. "Yes, you're going to try a new place to live and a new school."

She laughs, pulling away and twirling around. "This will be so much better."

"I hope so, hon. I hope so. Now, let's get you packed. We're due over there tomorrow in the early afternoon."

She grins. "I can't wait."

26

JACKLYN

I call Irena to check in and see how her daughter is doing. Irena answers, and she sounds out of breath, like she's in a hurry, which is normal for her. Everything is rush, rush, rush, and racing around, rescuing boats in distress.

I say, "Hi, I just wanted to see how you're both doing. And I wanted to thank you again for taking me to Shore Lodge on Christmas Eve day during a storm."

She laughs. "It was my pleasure, and it turned out to be a crazy, wild ride. Until I got home and found Kelly was gone." She lowers her voice and says, "I'm relieved she's home, but she isn't the same child. She refuses to go to school, because kids are teasing her about being different."

"Oh, no. That's awful. She's fabulous, but the other students don't see it?"

"That's right, and we have to make some changes to make her life better. Jack, Abby and I have agreed to let her live on Grand Island on a trial basis."

My arms jerk, and my dog wakes up, blinking his beautiful brown eyes at me. "Are you serious? Where will Kelly live? And what about school? Can you handle being away from her that long?"

"I have no idea if I can handle it, but she really wants this to happen, so we're making an effort. I wish we could go back, redo the past and stop my dad from taking her. It's my fault anyway, for not coming home right away on Christmas Eve day, after we docked. I shouldn't have gone to Karina's café and hung out with the rest of you. If I'd gone home from the boat, I might've stopped my father from forcing her into the car."

I shake my head. "That's a mighty big burden to carry by yourself, and if I were you, I'd set it down. We can't know if that would've changed things. If you'd come home earlier that day, maybe he would've picked her up from school one afternoon instead and kidnapped her another time. We don't get redo's, so let it go."

She sighs. "Thanks. I needed to hear that. Listen, I have to get going. We're packing up Kelly's things to take to Grand Island tomorrow. Want to join us?"

I blink with surprise. "Why sure. I'd love to be included." An idea crosses my mind. "Would it be okay if I brought along a neighbor friend who is having some troubles? I bet she'd like a break from being at home and living next door to her husband's ex-wife, who is over all the time. It's wearing on her nerves."

Irena says, "That's weird, the ex-wife lives next door?"

"Yes."

"I wouldn't put up with that. But is the ex an okay kind of person? Is she great to hang out with?"

I shake my head. "No, I don't think that's the case here. My neighbor's name is Jenna, and she lives two doors down from me. Her husband's ex was the one feeding raccoons, which led to our raccoon infestation."

"That was insane, with twenty raccoons around your place, staring at you."

I grip the phone tight. "Actually, there were twenty-four raccoons. And it was creepy, like in a Hitchcock movie, with more and more of them gathering and watching us. When one attacked Buddy, that was it. I drew the line." Hearing his name, my dog looks up at me, and I pet his soft ears.

She says, "I can see why. The poor dog. I'm glad he's okay."

"That problem has been solved, at least for now. I'll see you tomorrow. Meet you at the boat? And what time?"

"Be at the boat at noon tomorrow. Wear warm clothes and bring rain gear. I always like having you on board, because you know your way around boats. You're a good second mate."

"Thanks. I'll talk to Jenna and see if she wants to go. See you then. Should I bring food?"

"No, this will be an in and out, get there, meet and greet, and turn around trip. I'll chat with the teacher, and we'll be on our way back home before you know it."

I hang up and stand by the window. looking out into the night. I can't see much but tree branches blowing in the wind. It might be a bumpy ride tomorrow, but I'll be fine plowing through rough seas. I'm not sure about Jenna though. We might want snacks underway, and Karina's delicious scones from her café would taste wonderful. But I scuttle the idea of bringing scones, because Irena told me not to bring food, and she probably wouldn't want crumbs dropped in her wheelhouse. Like many skippers, she keeps her boat shipshape at all times.

I head to the kitchen and open a cupboard, pulling out a gift from my friend Mercury. The cardboard carton is heavy, and I open the box, smiling at gold-wrapped chocolate bars with chewy caramel and nuts. I'll take some tomorrow to share, because it doesn't seem right to hop onboard empty-handed, especially when I'm carrying the burden of guilt from keeping Irena away from her daughter on Christmas Eve day. While Irena was taking us on her boat to Shore Lodge to rescue four sane residents admitted to a secure psychiatric unit by family, unbeknownst to us, Kelly was about to be kidnapped.

I shake my head at how the horrible turn of events played out during a winter storm. With Irena's help, I confronted my demons at Shore Lodge, gave my friends a chance to escape, because there is nothing worse than being trapped, and we raced back to the marina, celebrating at the café afterwards. But by the time Irena arrived home, her daughter was gone.

Staring at the empty coffee maker, my mind drifts to my son, who is in Shore Lodge. I admitted him after he was injured in an avalanche. At some point, I'll take the ferry over to Cedar Island to visit him, but I'm not ready to face my manipulative, malicious, betraying son yet.

Picking up the phone, I call Jenna. When she answers, I say, "I'm going on a boat ride tomorrow with my friend Irena, and you're welcome to come along. Would you like to go to Grand Island with us?"

Jenna says in a low voice, "Yes, I need to get out of this house for my sanity. Where are we going and how long will we be gone?"

"Come to my place at eleven-thirty, and we'll meet at Irena's boat at noon. We're taking Irena's daughter, Kelly, to Grand Island to go to school there. The trip should take a few hours, but the weather can change on a dime, so wear warm clothes and bring a rain jacket and hat."

"Thanks. It sounds like fun. See you then."

We hang up, and I say to my sweet dog, "You'll need Mercury to check on you tomorrow."

I call Mercury, and he picks up, saying, "How's life over there?"

I smile, hearing his warm voice. "Fine, and I'm going on a boat ride tomorrow with Irena."

"Again? You just went out with her Christmas Eve day."

"I did, but Kelly is going to try going to school on Grand Island."

"Do they even have a school there?"

"Yes, they do. It's not big, but it has one teacher for kids of all ages."

"Are you sure Kelly will get a good education that way?"

I shrug. "It's not my choice, but Jack, Abby and Irena all agreed to it. Kelly is unhappy here in town, and it's her idea."

"That's a big change for a teenage girl, going from a small town to a one-room schoolhouse. Do you need me to watch Buddy while you're gone?"

"Would you, please? I'd appreciate it, and he likes you. It would be great if you could take him on a walk and hang around reading while I'm gone, if you're not busy."

"I can do that. Did you check the weather forecast? Strong winds are expected tomorrow. I hope you won't get stuck on Grand Island overnight."

I cringe. "I hope not, but it'll be good to get out in the fresh air and be on the water. I think my neighbor will like it too."

"Your neighbor is going? What's she got to do with Kelly and Irena?"

"Nothing, but it's a pressure cooker in her house, now

that her husband's ex-wife is living next door and popping over all the time."

"Remember when we talked about not meddling in the neighbors' lives?"

I tilt my head. "We did discuss that. But I decided to do something different and support Jenna during this trying time."

"Don't get dragged into their mess, or you might regret it. They might change their minds and turn on you."

I roll my eyes. "They'd never do that. They're nice people."

"We can always hope. What time do you want me to come over?"

"We'll be gone just before noon, so if you could let yourself in and take care of Buddy about two, that would be great. I'll take him on a walk at eleven, so he should be fine until then. It's too bad I can't take him on the boat, but we don't have room."

"I bet he'd rather be home sleeping and watching squirrels than boating. A boat ride might be rough on his stomach."

"I'm sorry I didn't invite you, instead of Jenna, on the trip."

"Always the last one on the list, am I?"

"No, you know that's not true, and I appreciate you. I just didn't think you'd enjoy a boat ride. And I needed you to take care of Buddy, so I guess I'm using you."

He chuckles. "Use me all you like. And I enjoy boat

rides. Someday, I'll tell you about when I helped a friend take his boat down the coast to Mexico."

"I'd like to hear about that. Goodnight and thanks for taking care of Buddy. I'll text you when we're coming back to town."

"Stay safe out there."

We hang up, and I say to Buddy, "Mercury will watch over you tomorrow, while I'm on the high seas with Irena. Don't you worry, I'll get home safely."

He jumps off the couch and shakes, tags clanking, and goes to the door. I open it, and he runs out into the back yard and does his business, stopping to sniff grass. Cold air blows inside, making me shiver, and I call, "Buddy, come. Let's go."

He trots inside, and I close the door. He sits in the kitchen, eying me, and I give him a dog treat. "Good boy. We had our walk, and a stop at the fractious neighbors' house, and you did your business, so it's time to head to bed."

I double check the door locks and turn off the lights, shuddering when I recall how Dusty broke in at night with another man, who remains in jail for the crime. My son blamed his friend for planning the home invasion, but I know better. Mercury and Del helped me repair the door frame and door, but what a heinous crime that was, frightening me to my core and scaring my dog. The worst of it was, the act was committed by a family member.

I shuffle down the hall, followed by Buddy, and brush

my teeth, slipping into bed and pulling the covers up to my chin. But sleep evades me, and I blink in the dark. I know what to do with Albert's ashes now, but what will I do about Stone Estates? Is it wrong to drop a project and not follow through with Albert's plans, veering from his intentions?

Rolling over on my side, I release a sigh. Albert wouldn't want to burden me with his expectations, hopes and dreams. The path to building a subdivision has become too troublesome. I was feeling obligated to adhere to a dead man's wishes, but now I realize I don't need to build big homes on a hill above town. I'm free to do what I like with the property and for the rest of my life.

I nod. The dream Albert and Dusty wove is officially dead on this dark night for many reasons. The price of lumber went sky high. Interest rates soared. A secured loan on my home would mean I'd have to give up my house if the project flopped. The environmental survey results mean I have a smaller space to build and place utilities and sewer lines. Besides, if I step back, the concept of building mega homes, like Dusty and Albert envisioned, is not one I embrace. Times have changed, and so have I, since they roughed out plans.

I own the land outright, so I could sell it to a developer or donate it to a nature conservation group. But I won't donate it, because I need the money from the land to fund my retirement, after Dusty raided my bank accounts and sold my garden store when I was locked in Shore Lodge.

From here on in, what I do is my choice, with no strings attached to my dear, departed husband who deceived me by giving our son money behind my back.

I whisper, "Onward, ho," and close my eyes, imagining a new future for the plot of land looking west to the San Juan Islands. I could create a retreat center, build tiny homes and a huge fenced dog park. With a sigh, I welcome sleep and let the currents of my mind flow with ideas as I drift away on dreams.

27

IRENA

y hands tremble as I help Kelly pack her favorite things. When two suitcases are full, we close them and flop down on the bed on our backs, side by side, staring at the ceiling. Clearing my throat, I say, "I can't believe this is happening, and you're going across the water, away from me."

She slips her hand into mine and says, "I can't believe it either. But it hurts too much to live here. Everything in this house reminds me of when Granddad took me. He was nice when I first met him, before he turned into a monster."

I pull her into my arms. "Sweet girl, I'm so sorry that happened to you. I've been trying so hard to protect you all along, but I failed you at a crucial time. I should have been home, not out on the boat with Jacklyn."

She sighs. "Thanks for saying that."

I pat her arm and sit up. "But now you're getting the chance you wanted. You're moving from one island to another, at least for a while, and not everyone gets to do that. I'd say you're pretty special in my book, valentine."

I grin at her, and she groans. "Stop, Mom, you're sounding corny. Let's just pretend this is like every other night. Otherwise, if we talk about it, it'll freak me out."

I stand, putting my hands on my hips. "Should we have hot chocolate with marshmallows on top?"

She jumps up and smiles. "Yes, and I'll make it. It's my last night here for a bit."

I point a finger. "But you're coming home to visit, remember that. And I'll still be your mother, no matter what, wherever you are."

She nods and hurries down the hall to the kitchen. I swallow a lump in my throat and follow her, fiddling with my fingers. I'm not sure what my future holds without my daughter under my roof. Who am I without Kelly by my side most moments? I'll have to figure that out.

28

JENNA

I rummage through my dresser, opening drawers, and pick out clothes to wear on the boat trip tomorrow. I want to escape from my house. Zoila and Kirk are making eyes at each other under my nose, as if I don't exist.

Biting my lower lip, I reflect that our neighborhood is too small for the three of us. This town isn't big enough. If she moved across the world, it wouldn't be far enough away for my liking.

Kirk comes in the bedroom, leaning against the door frame and watching me pick out clothes. His stony silence must mean he isn't pleased with how I'm acting toward his ex-wife, but I don't care. I've had enough.

In a sarcastic tone of voice, I say, "Is Zoila enjoying herself, soaking in our tub?"

He frowns and folds his arms. "You should get over it."

I grimace and toss my long underwear, jeans and a sweater on a chair by the window. "I'm not happy about this, not one bit. Right now, she should be in the house next door, where she belongs, taking a bath there. I won't have her living here, and I can't believe you invited her, without talking to me first. You invited the woman who wants you back in her arms to move in with us, which is totally unacceptable. And, I'll remind you, this is my house. I get final say."

His eyes open wide. "She's lonely and needs friends. And this is our place. We're married."

Putting my hands on my hips, I see him in a new light. He's on her side and not taking my feelings into account. I swallow bitter bile laced with betrayal and say, "She doesn't want to make friends with me. She's clinging to you and pushing us apart."

He looks over his shoulder, as if checking to see if Zoila is hovering close by, and a worried look crosses his face. Stepping close, he says in a low voice, "I can't tell you exactly what's going on, but I have to help her. I can't get out of it, but this whole thing isn't how it looks. I love you. You've got to believe me."

I snort. "Nice try, but I don't believe you. It's her or me, and you have to pick between us. I won't be the third wheel, like I was tonight in my own home."

Zoila sashays into the room, swaying her hips and smiling. "I couldn't help but overhear you two talking. I just wanted to say I'm going next door to sleep tonight, but

I can't wait to move in tomorrow. So long, you two." She wiggles her long fingers, waving goodbye.

I step out of our bedroom and watch her take one step at a time, holding on to the handrail. For a flash, I picture her falling to the bottom of the staircase, landing in a heap, never to rise again. It would be satisfying, to see her rid from our lives. Scratching the back of my neck, I shake my head. What kind of monster have I become to wish for her death?

Zoila looks up. "Kirk? Would you please come help me? I need your help getting down the stairs. I might trip and fall, and I don't want that to happen, because then I'd have to sue you. You wouldn't want that, would you?"

Kirk hurries to her side, and she takes his arm. My hands clench, as they go slowly, step by step, down the stairs. He gives me a quick glance but turns his attention to her, and she whispers in his ear. They laugh together on the last step, and their voices fade away as they walk outside.

Closing the bedroom door, I lean back against it and tears trickle down my cheeks. Wind whooshes past the house, and I tap my lips. Before I married Kirk, a woman at work said, "You should get him to sign a quit claim deed to your house in Millersville, so that no matter what happens, it will always be yours. You've got to protect yourself, in case you guys split up."

At the time, I shook my head and shrugged it off, feeling insulted that she'd thrown a dark shadow on our upcoming marriage. But now her words ring in my head, sounding wise in hindsight. I'm in the midst of an unthinkable moment, with Kirk assuming I'm fine with his ex-wife moving into my home, and I must take action. I'll get him to sign the quit claim deed, and if he continues to insist on Zoila living here, I'll boot them both out.

The furnace kicks on, but I'm chilled to the bone. I don't want our marriage to end, but the stark reality of my living situation is untenable. If I go along with the flow, I'll be pulled under and drown. My dad always said to hope for the best and prepare for the worst, and this is definitely a time to arm myself for battle.

I hurry down the stairs to my study. Closing the door, I open my laptop and go online, researching and printing out a quit claim deed for Kirk to sign. I head into the kitchen for a drink of water but stop at the sink, glass in hand, and freeze when movement in the house next door catches my attention.

Zoila wraps her arms around Kirk's neck. My mouth falls open, and I flick off the kitchen lights. My husband leans into her, patting her back. He smiles.

My body is still as a statue. My heart thuds, and my hands turn cold.

I cross my arms and whisper into the cold, dark night, "You may think you've won, but I'm not a doormat. Just you wait."

29

ZOILA

We walk into the house I'm renting next door, and I slump on the sofa, touching my back. "My hips ache. Will you massage where it hurts?"

Kirk's eyebrows knit together, and he rests a hand on the doorknob. "I've got to go home and talk with Jenna. She's really upset."

I pout, pushing my lips out. "You know I need more help than her, don't you? I'm the one who is sick. She doesn't have cancer, like I do."

He scratches his stubbled chin. "Sure, I know that. But she's my wife. I've got to be fair to her."

I wave a hand in the air. "She knows you love her. She doesn't need reassurance." I pat the couch cushion. "Come over here and sit down. Let's talk about our future and what I have planned for us."

His jaw drops. "What're you talking about? There is no future for you and me. Mine is with Jenna. We're just helping you out while you're getting medical treatment."

"Come sit. I'll explain everything."

He runs a hand through his hair. "No thanks, I've got to get back before she blows a fuse. She's really ticked off. Come to think of it, I don't know if it's such a good idea for you to move in with us."

I let a tear slide down my cheek. Sniffing, I wipe it away and go over to him, slipping my arms around his neck. He stands still as stone, and I say, "You can't change your mind now. I already put in the change of address form at the post office. We'll all live together. It'll be fun."

He barely pats my back, so I step back and open my eyes wide, blinking at him and telling myself to do better. It was a lame excuse I manufactured on the spot about my mail. I've got to up my game to pull this off.

Giving me a grim smile, he shakes his head. "You can't manipulate me by crying. Not this time. I want to save my marriage, if I still can."

I tilt my head and stick out a hip. "You didn't bother to save your first marriage. You let yourself be lured away by the temptress next door. Shame on you for leaving me in the lurch and divorcing me to be with Jenna. Our friends sided with you, no one wanted to see me, and I was all alone. You left me with nothing. No friends. No husband. No money. You made me sick and get cancer. You did this to me."

He opens his hands. "Come on, I didn't give you cancer. It just happened. It's not my fault you're sick, so don't put that on me. And you were working, so you were able to pay rent. You could have kept in contact with our friends and made new ones. But no, you wanted to be a victim, and you play your role well. Hats off to you for getting me to pay your rent and medical bills, but this is where it stops. I've changed my mind, and I don't want you to move in. I've got to go."

I jab a finger at his face. "You're not calling the shots, I am. You can't get out of this. We have an agreement."

He opens the door, hurries out and doesn't look back. I run to the door and call, "Wait, come back. Remember the things that I know."

But he hurries into his house and closes the door. I frown at the sound of the lock snicking shut. He may think he can block me out, but I'm smarter than he is. I'll finagle a way to get closer and create havoc, siphoning off more money before they realize what is happening.

Closing my front door, I gaze into their house, where they're waving their hands in the air and pointing fingers at each other. They're at each other's throats, so my plan is working. I'll check that off the list and move on to the next step, gaining access to their computers, passwords and bank accounts.

I watch the show going on next door and smile when Jenna holds up a piece of paper in the air. I say in soft voice, "I have much more in store for you. It's payback time, and you'll finally get what you deserve."

30

KIRK

I break free from Zoila and hurry to my home, running up the front steps. I'm out of breath by the time I step inside and lock the door. Jenna sits in a chair by the cold fireplace. Wind blows through the broken window. No one has cleaned up the shards of glass, which I hoped she'd do while I was next door. Jenna stands and walks over to me, holding a piece of paper.

I move in to give her a hug, like we always do when one of us comes home, but she steps out of my arms and frowns. I can't help but glance next door, where Zoila is standing in the window, watching us. What an idiot I was to move her into the house next door. I hope Jenna won't notice we have an audience.

I swallow to clear the guilt stuck at the back of my throat. "Are you upset? Tell me. I want to hear all about it."

In a loud voice, she says, "What do you think? Do I look upset to you?"

I hold up my hands. "All right, I'm sorry. Of course you're upset."

She crosses her arms, grasping a piece of white paper with something printed on it. Rubbing my chin, I hope she's not filing for divorce. While I was next door, she could have gone online and printed out one of those do-it-yourself divorce forms, like I did with Zoila. The pasta and cake I ate churn in my gut, and bile creeps up my throat.

Her eyes narrow. "I'm tempted to kick you to the curb."

I say in a quiet voice, "I hope you don't mean that, because I love you, and we're good together. Who would I have morning coffee with?"

She tilts her head. "Your girlfriend would be more than happy to take my place."

"I know I've been wrong, but I'll make it up to you. I promise I will."

She shakes her head. "You'll have to do better than that. You've been treating me worse than you would a dog. Tomorrow, we'll go a notary and if you sign this document, I might give our marriage another try. If not, you're out tonight, and you can sleep next door."

My voice trembles when I say, "What is it?"

She marches over to the dining room table and slaps it down. "It's a quit claim deed to surrender all rights to my house that I owned before we were married."

My mouth hangs open. "Surrender my rights? But

we're married. Whatever is mine is yours, and the other way around. Are you saying what I think you're saying?"

She taps a finger on the white piece of paper with black printed words. "What I'm saying is, if you sign this in front of a notary tomorrow with Mary, Jacklyn's friend, then I'll give us another chance. But she can't move in. Otherwise, yes, I'll file for divorce."

I gasp and rest a hand on my sour belly. "Surely, you don't mean that. I've just been helping out a friend. There's nothing wrong with that."

Her brown eyes bore into me. "Everything is wrong with how you two flirt and touch each other and act like you're in love. I'm sick of it. Put a stop to her being in our lives while I'm on the boat tomorrow."

I shake my head. "I'm just helping a sick friend."

"Do you think I'm an idiot? She wants to be more than your friend. I can tell from how she acts, and you're soaking up her attention like a sponge. You've got to cut her off."

I run a hand through my hair. "I can't. I'm trapped."

"Figure it out tomorrow while I'm on the boat, because I'm done being nice. Here's the document for you to look over."

I take the paper with a trembling hand, caught with these lies hemming me in. I blurt out, "I'll sign. But I wish you weren't so harsh about this."

She gives me a death glare. "That was not a smart thing to say. I don't know who you are anymore."

"I'm sorry."

Pressing my lips together, I read the document and nod, realizing by signing it, I release any claims to this house. I'm in a vise, caught between two women, and it's my fault. I loved Jenna and hoped we could deal with Zoila. But I was wrong, and I've gone too far with this charade. Things aren't working out how I thought they would.

She taps a toe. "If you don't go with me to sign this and get it notarized tomorrow, our marriage is dead."

My mouth goes dry. I've been using Jenna's income to pay for Zoila's medical treatments, so I've got to keep her happy, so she won't get suspicious and check our bank account. When Zoila moved next door, I suggested that I take over paying our household bills, and Jenna was delighted to relinquish the responsibility.

Swallowing hard, I say, "Okay, I'll sign it tomorrow."

She whips the paper away, tucking it under her arm. Her gaze travels to Zoila, standing in front of her window, arms crossed and observing us. What a fool I was to play with fire by moving Zoila in next door.

Jenna turns and stomps away, taking the quit claim deed with her. I've got to patch things up with her and send Zoila out of our lives. I suppress a groan, because I've been an idiot, basking in Zoila's praise and being in her alluring arms.

My gaze catches on Zoila, who motions for me to come to the window. Cold air rushes past, making hairs on my neck stand on end. Zoila points upstairs in her house and smiles. With a shudder, I turn away before I burst into flames. She's trouble, and I knew it, but I went ahead anyway with her plan. I can only blame myself if everything falls apart.

A curtain by the broken window blows in the wind. Blowing out a breath, I shuffle to the kitchen and grab a broom and dustpan. As I sweep up shards of glass, Zoila's voice calls in the wind. "Kirk, come over. I have a surprise for you."

I shake my head, grit my teeth and bend down, getting to work to repair the damage Zoila did.

31

JACKLYN

Tucking six gold foil wrapped chocolate bars into a small backpack in the morning, I sip my second cup of strong black coffee. I let out a sigh and hope things will go well for Kelly on Grand Island at her new school. Sitting at the kitchen table, I glance at my red long underwear worn under khaki shorts with hiking boots. Kelly likes the way that I dress, and I'm looking forward to seeing her today.

I set the cup in the sink and go in the bathroom to brush my teeth and floss, hoping to keep plaque and dementia at bay, because my dental hygienist says bacteria on teeth can cause gum disease associated with Alzheimer's disease. Good grief, we have to worry about everything these days, including bacteria getting into our brains. I miss the days when we knew less and bumbled along, thinking we knew everything but knowing little, not realizing what lurked in the dark.

I gear up to take Buddy for a walk before I leave with Jenna. Zipping up my puffer coat, I leash up Buddy and say, "I'm going to meet Irena at the marina. Doesn't that sound good, sweet pup?"

I chuckle at how it rhymes and say, "I'll meet Irena at the marina." Buddy gives me a glance, as if to say, "I have many sniffs to smell. Let's go."

We step outside, and a stiff breeze blows by. Misty fog gives off a morning chill, and I pull down my wool black watch cap after locking the door. I'm in the habit of securing my home, even though my primary nemesis, my son, is in a secure ward at Shore Lodge.

Ship horns blast five times, altering other vessels of their location in the fog. I wince because this does not bode well for our upcoming boat journey today. A wispy white veil of fog drifts past.

A man steps out of Jenna's house, slamming the door behind him, and trots down the front steps, coming toward me. Buddy growls. The man stops, hands clenched at his sides, and stares at me.

I blink at the angry, glaring, haggard man before I recognize him. Dark circles under his eyes make him look like he hasn't slept for days. "Oh, hi Kirk. You look different. I didn't think it was you."

"Jacklyn, I hate to butt in on your friendship with Jenna, but you've got to cancel the boat trip or tell Jenna it's off. She's up there getting ready, and I don't want her to go."

I tilt my head. "Why not?"

He clears his throat. "To be honest, I think you've become a bad influence on her, and she isn't acting like herself."

I snort. "I hope you're joking."

He hitches up his pants. "I'm not. I'm dead serious."

"I haven't told her anything to do."

He fists his hands. "It's not what you're saying. You're leading by example. You're independent, and it's wearing off on her."

I tip my head back in the foggy mist and laugh. "Thank you for paying me a compliment. I appreciate it. Now, I'll be on my way."

Jenna comes out of the house with a briefcase in her hands. "Come on," she says to Kirk, "Mary is expecting us. We'll get this notarized before the boat trip, then we'll go out to dinner when I get home. And by dinner, I mean just the two of us, without Zoila. Am I clear?"

He pulls his maroon cardigan sweater close and follows Jenna to the car. I hurry on my way and say to Buddy under my breath, "They've got a lot going on, don't they? I hope they'll work it out."

32

JENNA

My muscles tense as I drive to the notary's house. Last night, I didn't sleep much. I was worried that if I didn't get the document signed and notarized today, Kirk would balk and it would be impossible to drag him to Mary's house after the boat trip.

I drum on the steering wheel, and the urge to take action swims through my veins. I want to keep what I inherited, and with Zoila sniffing around the edges, I'm worried Kirk will cave, let her move into my home and cater to her whims, including letting her dip into our finances. My having this quit claim deed document will set the tone and stop the madness. Otherwise, I have a feeling Kirk will cave, and I'll spend the rest of my life with Zoila in my face.

Kirk says, "I don't see why this is necessary. You should trust me. I can't believe you want to do this."

I park out front of Mary's one-story house. "Come on," I say, getting out and pointing past the picket fence. "I brought the house into our marriage, so this document makes that fact clear."

He climbs out of the car. "Okay, but I don't like being pushed into something."

I glance at him as we go up the front walk. "But you've pushed me into seeing your ex-wife every day since she moved in. I miss it being only the two of us."

He pats my back, but instead of a gentle touch, it's more of a thwack. I grit my teeth and stop myself from flinching. What a difference a few months makes, living through a certain ex constantly coming over, knocking and ringing the doorbell. The sound of the bell or a knock on the door makes me jump these days, and my heart races.

Before I can knock, Mary swings open the door and smiles. Gesturing inside, she says, "Come on in out of the cold." She's wearing a paint-smudged smock, with a smear of yellow paint on her cheek.

We step inside, and she says, "Can I get you anything? Coffee, water or tea?"

Kirk stomps his feet and frowns. "No, we'll just get my signature notarized, and we'll be on our way home."

Mary looks from me to Kirk, as if questioning why we're together, which is exactly what has been running through my head. Perhaps he always been this abrupt, but I didn't notice, Or, more likely, he's changed, under the spell of Zoila, the temptress.

I say to Mary, "Thanks for meeting us on short notice. I appreciate it."

She says, "Any friend of Jacklyn's is a friend of mine."

Kirk's back stiffens beside me.

She points. "Follow me. We'll go in the kitchen."

We sit at a round table. The kitchen has an orange counter top and wallpaper decorated with cooking utensils and pots and pans. The countertops are cluttered. I nod, because this feels like a home, not just a house, and Mary radiates a feeling of love.

She takes the quit claim deed from me and reads it over, nodding. "This looks good. It is a simple, straight forward legal document. Sign in this ledger, and I'll notarize it."

She slides a notary ledger over to Kirk, and he enters his name and address and signature. She pulls out a seal and notarizes the document. "That's all there is to it. Do you have my fee?"

"Oh, that's right. Just a minute." I dig in a pocket and pull out a credit card, but she shakes her head. "That won't work. I'm not as fancy as that. It'll have to be cash or a check."

My cheeks heat, because I forgot to bring cash or a check. Kirk whips a checkbook out of his back pocket and takes a pen off the table. "I'll pay. We're married after all, and it's our money."

I study him, because he doesn't look like the man I fell for. But I've changed as well. Aging isn't in the flattery business, and wrinkles around my eyes are more evident.

He peers in his checkbook, and his eyes widen, but at what, I don't know. Did he make a mistake adding things up? Or did awful Zoila dip her finger tips into our stash of cash? I dearly hope not. When I get home from the boat trip, I'll double-check our bank accounts.

He rips out a check and hands it to her. "There you go."

She stands. "Thank you."

I slide the notarized document into my briefcase, and we walk out.

He offers me a stiff smile. "That's done. Onto the rest of the day."

I nod. "Thanks, let's go out to dinner tonight."

"I'd like that."

His phone rings, and he answers, but when he hears who it is, his eyes grow wide. He says to whoever is calling, "I can't talk now." He hangs up and shoves his phone in his pocket.

We climb in the car, and I turn toward home, saying, "Was that Zoila?"

He's quiet for a beat, so I say, "It's okay, you can tell me. We have to be honest with each other."

He nods. "Yeah, that was Z."

"What did she want?"

"She wants me to come over to fix a dripping faucet."

My grip tightens on the wheel. "Uh huh."

"I know you don't like it when I help her, but it's the right thing to do."

I stop myself from rolling my eyes at how persistent she is. Parking in our driveway, I turn to him and say, "I've got to head to the boat with Jacklyn. You deal with the situation however you think is best."

33

IRENA

I'm waiting at the marina with the boat engine warmed up when Jacklyn and Jenna stride down the dock, coats rippling in the breeze. They say hello to Kelly, who waits on the dock, and step on board.

I say, "Sit down and make yourselves at home. The trip won't take too long."

Kelly sticks her head in the wheelhouse. "She means it'll take an hour or so on the way over. Mom, okay if I release the lines"

"Yes, go ahead, release the lines, and we'll get underway."

"Roger that." She tosses the lines on the dock. "The lines are off."

"Here we go." I pull away from the dock and putter at five knots through the marina, avoiding creating a wake. Kelly comes in the wheelhouse and sits down.

When we're beyond the breakwater., I push on the throttle, and we roar around the tip of Cap Sante, heading north to Cedar Channel. Wisps of fog drift past, and I strain my eyes, keeping a careful lookout for submerged logs ahead.

Kelly stands. "Fog's getting thicker."

I nod. "Check the radar for boats coming our way."

"Got it."

Jacklyn grips a hand hold and instructs Jenna to hold on tight. Turning west into Cedar Channel, our speed slows, because we're running against the current.

Jenna says, "Why did we slow down?"

Jacklyn says, "We're opposing the current."

"Does it always run the same way?"

I chime in. "No, it changes all the time."

"Sounds confusing."

I shrug. "It's a challenge, but it's fun to figure it out. I could increase our speed, but in this fog, I'd rather not. Best to keep a close watch in conditions like this."

"I am," Kelly says.

Jacklyn goes over and pats Kelly's back. "I bet you're excited. It's a big change for you and a giant leap into the unknown. Like grafting a new type of apple to a branch."

Kelly grins. "I'm excited. I hope it works out."

Jacklyn says, "Was it difficult to pick out what to take with you?"

Kelly shrugs. "Not really. I don't wear many clothes,

just the same ones. Mom, will you look after my Dicken's books while I'm gone?"

We enter Rosario Strait, where the fog is thick. Ship horns blast around us, and I head toward Thatcher Pass. "I will. Hey, watch the radar, will you? What's that blip moving closer to us on the port side?"

Kelly says in a tight voice, "It might be a fast-moving speed boat. They're heading right for us."

"That's what I thought. Hold on everyone, we're taking evasive maneuvers." I veer off course, swing the wheel over and the dot grows larger on the radar, but is now going parallel to us and not aiming at our midships. Out of the white wispy gloom, a metal fishing boat appears, flying over waves, cutting through fog.

I grit my teeth and hold a course away from a certain collision with the fast boat.

In a flash, the boat moves past us and is gone, disappearing like a ghost, swallowed up by dense fog. I whoosh out a breath and wipe my brow with the back of my hand, checking the radar for vessels in the area and turning the wheel back on course for Thatcher Pass.

A loud horn blast sounds behind us. Jacklyn jumps in the air. Jenna flinches and squeals, but Kelly and I smile. I glance out the stern at a large ferry boat, approaching and coming up fast, and turn the wheel, steering closer to land.

Kelly points to the stern. "It's a ferry boat. Doesn't it look huge?"

Jenna stares, ogling the big, beamy boat. "Wow."

Jacklyn says, "Kelly, you could take over for your mom someday, running the rescue boat business. You know your way around boats so well."

Kelly gives her a shy smile. "Thanks, but I want to do something else. Mom works all the time."

I sigh and hope one day my daughter will change her mind. Not everyone is cut out to run a rescue boat business, dealing with drama on the high seas, but I have a feeling she would be a natural.

Jenna says, "How long until we get there?"

I cock my head. "About thirty to forty minutes."

The marine radio erupts with a call. "Mayday, mayday, mayday. This is a thirty-four-foot powerboat Alice. Another boat hit us, and we're taking on water. Can anyone rescue us?"

34

JENNA

Irena slows the boat's speed and says, "Sorry, Kelly, I know you want to get to the island, but if no one else jumps in to help them, we have to take this call."

Kelly nods. "I understand. Roger that."

Waves splash up the sides of the boat. The smell of salt air wafts through the wheelhouse. We're socked in by fog, with white wisps around us. Irena reaches up for the marine radio microphone and steers.

I chew the inside of my cheek, worrying about my rocky marriage and boaters in trouble. Jacklyn stares at the gray choppy water. Kelly squirms in her seat. Seconds stretch like hours in the silent wheelhouse.

A man's voice comes over the marine radio. "Mayday, mayday, mayday. This is the powerboat Alice. We're taking on water. Can anyone help us?"

Irena keys the microphone and says, "Alice, this is the rescue boat Nimbus. What's your position?"

"I'm not sure. A metal fishing boat hit us off the south end of Cypress Island."

"Roger that, Alice. We'll double back and come help you. Stay on this channel, and we'll alert you when we're on the scene."

I watch open-mouthed at the smooth precision of Irena's executed turn as she works the marine radio and the wheel. We're quiet on the boat, straining our eyes to see through dense fog.

Irena says, "Jacklyn, watch the radar for incoming boats. Call out if there's a concern."

Jacklyn focuses on the radar. "Got it."

"Kelly," Irena says, "make sure we're all wearing life vests and prepare to come alongside the other boat. I'll see if I can stop the boat from sinking. If not, we'll take on passengers. We have to move fast."

My pulse picks up, because our fun boat outing just become a race against death. I joined Jacklyn and her friends to have a breather, but conflict and danger lurk everywhere. When I get home, I'll take control of my living situation, instead of letting Zoila ruin my life and manipulate my husband. A glimmer of hope might remain to save my marriage. I'll insist Zoila come over less often, draping her arms around Kirk's neck.

I frown and wonder if separating Zoila physically from my husband will dampen her charms. A lump forms in my throat, and I swallow tears. I have the feeling I'm missing a key piece to the puzzle about Kirk and his former wife. They know something that I don't. I can sense it when the three of us are together.

Irena speaks into the microphone. "Alice, Alice, Alice, this is Nimbus. How many people are on board? Are you all wearing personal floatation devices?"

"Four people, and no, we're not wearing life jackets."

"Put on the life jackets and get ready to abandon ship. How much water is onboard now?"

"We have four inches of water onboard, maybe more."

"What about the fishing boat that hit you? Are they sinking too?"

"No, they're fine. The metal fishing boat was going fast, and they're heading back to the marina."

Irena sets down the microphone and shakes her head. "The boat that flew by us earlier might've hit Alice. If we hadn't changed course, they would've rammed into us."

I shudder and fold my arms. My jaunt on the water has become an exciting journey. I hope we'll get to the boat in distress before it sinks.

Biting my lower lip, I wonder what my husband is doing at this moment. Is he telling her off? Or did he cave and go over to fix her faucet? Maybe he went for a walk to clear his head. Or, maybe he's in Zoila's bed.

My stomach knots. Kirk and I had been happy until his ex-wife tracked us down. Like this boat we're racing towards, our relationship is sinking, and I'm not sure I want to save it. I may have reached the breaking point, given his puppy eyes adoration of his ex-wife.

I let out a sigh and hope he'll have straightened out the situation and extricated himself from her grasp by the time I get home.

35

JACKLYN

Irena steers toward the boat in distress. We're quiet in the wheelhouse and grope our way through fog. Ship horns call out, bleating eerie sounds, near and far. Irena hunches over the helm and pushes on the throttle, as we hurry ahead.

Staring at the radar, I say, "No one's near us, at least for now."

Irena says, "Keep a close eye on it. The direction of the wind should change pretty soon to come from the north, if the forecast was right. That'll clear away the fog."

She looks over at Kelly. "How're you doing, hon?"

Kelly sighs. "I know we have to go help that boat, but I wanted to get settled in my new place."

"Sorry, sweetie. I wish we didn't have to turn back, but we do."

Kelly frowns. "It's that metal boat's fault for racing around in fog, causing an accident."

I shake my head. "Some boaters are idiots, and they drive like it's a race car, ignoring rules and being inconsiderate of others. I'd like to slap the most egregious ones with big fat fines."

Irena looks over. "Kelly, what does egregious mean?"

Kelly taps on her phone. "It means bad, shocking."

I smile. "Well, that can be our word of the day. Let's see how often we can use it."

The marine radio erupts. "This is the fishing vessel Alice. We're taking on water and need help."

Irena picks up the microphone and is about to speak when a woman's voice comes over the channel. "This is the United States Coast Guard hailing the fishing vessel Alice." A woman repeats the call three times.

I raise my eyebrows and glance at Irena.

Irena says to me, "It'd be great if the Coast Guard took this off our hands."

A man says over the radio, "This is the fishing boat Alice. Come in, Coast Guard."

"Alice, we have a Coast Guard cutter in position near you and can send a rigid inflatable to assist."

"Please do that."

"Confirming that, Alice. We are three minutes out. Put on your personal flotation devices. U.S. Coast Guard out."

Irena speaks into the marine radio microphone, "This is Nimbus, Nimbus, Nimbus. We are cancelling the call to assist the vessel Alice, and we are turning around."

"U.S. Coast Guard here. Confirming that, Nimbus. U.S. Coast Guard out."

Irena turns the boat around, resuming course. She grins. "We're back on track, heading to Grand Island, as planned."

Kelly beams. "Finally."

Jenna says, "I thought boating was easy. But there's a lot going on, isn't there?"

Irena stares at a ferry boat heading toward us. She turns the wheel, hugging the side of Thatcher Pass, giving the big, beamy boat enough space to safely pass. "Yep, lots is going on, but that's the fun, figuring it out."

Jenna tilts her head. "I was hoping to see whales."

"You might," I say, "watch for spotter planes circling one area, searching for them. Or a cluster of boats stopped in one place. That's often a sign of whales in the area."

Wind sweeps down from the north, blowing away wisps of white fog. Under a blue sky, we make our way to Grand Island and Kelly's new school.

I purse my lips. When we get back to the marina in Millersville, I'll drop off Jenna and shop at my former garden store for a tree to plant with Albert's ashes. It's time to move on with my life.

Tapping my lips, I wonder if I'm doing the right thing by jettisoning Albert's dreams for a fancy subdivision with high-end super-expensive swanky homes.

Irena says, "Jacklyn, you look deep in thought. Anything bothering you?"

Sunlight dances on choppy water. I nod. "I'm on the precipice of a big decision."

Kelly says, "What is it?"

"I'm about to let go of my plans to build Stone Estates."

Irena looks over at me. "But you loved the idea of building big, beautiful homes with gorgeous views. I wanted to buy one, but I knew I couldn't afford to live there."

I clear my throat. "I couldn't own one either, even at a deep discount. And with building costs going up and interest rates rising, I'm asking myself if that's what I really want to do with my time, energy and money. Besides, it's laden with risk, and I might go broke doing it."

Jenna says, "I understand being on the verge of a major decision. It's scary, and you're not sure you're making the right choice."

Gazing at forested land and a grand timbered home with a wide deck facing the water, I say, "My gut says to drop it like a red-hot poker, but I feel foolish, like I wasted money getting an environmental survey and applying for building permits."

Kelly says, "Do what you want. Don't worry about what others think."

I glance down at my red leggings and grin at her. "Thanks. I don't usually care about what other people think, but for some reason, this time, I do. I was all excited about my new venture and remaking myself along the way."

Irena's boat chugs forward, plowing through the Salish Sea. I wave to a little beach as we pass by. "Goodbye, Stone Estates. You were a good idea at one time, but now you're gone. Soon, you'll be in my rear-view mirror."

"Bye, bye, big homes." Kelly says.

"Bye," the others say.

A moment passes, and I say, "What was most egregious was what Dusty did when he broke into my home and brought along that other man. But Buddy saved me."

Irena glances over. "From what I've heard, you saved yourself."

A smile spreads across my face. "Grabbing a brass candlestick, I charged after them and tripped the tall one, who ended up being Dusty. He went down, and I tied him up before the police arrived. Buddy took care of the other guy."

Jenna raises her eyebrows. "Remind me not to get on your bad side."

"Nice work, Jacklyn," Irena says, focusing on the water ahead. "Is Dusty going to serve time for the home invasion at your house?"

"He missed his court appearance when he was in the avalanche, which is standard practice for him, shirking his responsibilities and going out on a wilderness trek instead of showing up in court. I'm not sure what's going to happen. But he blamed the other man, who is still serving time."

Irena says, "The poor guy. I heard he ran the grocery store in Foothills near the mountains. Now he's in jail, and he'll have a record for the rest of his life."

I sigh. "All because Dusty convinced him to do it. I can see Dusty dragging some unsuspecting person into his plan and pinning the blame on them. It wouldn't bother my son's conscience one bit."

Kelly says, "That's egregious."

The rest of us say, "It is."

36

JENNA

Going past forested islands, I mull over Jacklyn's decision to jettison her plans to build a subdivision. Watching her chat with Kelly, a flicker of worry flits through my mind. I hope by the time I arrive home Kirk will have come to his senses and moved Zoila out of our life. What a relief it will be to not have her stopping by several times a day, conjuring up excuses to bring Kirk next door. All last week, Kirk's phone dinged with texts, and when I asked him what was going on, he wouldn't meet my gaze and said he was working on something. He's never been secretive like that before.

Jacklyn comes over to me. "What's going on? Anything wrong?"

"I'm worried about how close Kirk is with Zoila."

Jacklyn nods. "I would be too. They're living out of each other's pockets."

I wince. "Can you believe this? She tried to move in my house last night to live with us, and Kirk told her it was fine, but I said no. I'm hoping Kirk will tell her off and move her far away while we're on the boat, and I'll come home and can relax in my own house. The moon wouldn't be far enough for my liking. I'm fed up. Every time I look out a window, there she is, watching us from her place. It's driving me nuts, having to live like this. I didn't marry her, I married Kirk."

Jacklyn cocks her head. "Maybe she wants to irritate you, and she's trying to drive a wedge between you and Kirk."

"I think you're right, but it's hard not to react and get upset when she's draping herself over my husband, and he's drooling."

"I was ready to strangle her at the dinner table, and I was only there a short time. I think even Buddy was put off by her."

I throw my hands up in the air. "She's a temptress, and it's Kirk's fault for inviting her to live next door and move in with us without checking with me first. That's crazy. No one does that."

Shaking my head, I say, "I suspect she has something big hanging over his head, but I don't know what it is. I've got to pretend their closeness doesn't bother me, because when I get upset, she looks happy, and I'm driving them closer together."

"That sounds about right. She seems smart."

"I think she got him to pay her rent, and we sure as heck can't afford that. I'll check our bank accounts when I get home, because maybe I've been too trusting."

Jacklyn's brows knit together. "Do that and soon. I waited too long and assumed everything was fine until it wasn't, and by the time I found out, the horse had left the barn long ago."

I lean in. "This might sound strange, but I don't think she's sick or getting chemotherapy. I'd like to find out if she's faking having cancer."

Jacklyn raises her eyebrows. "That's quite an accusation, and it'd be tough to find out, given patient confidentiality rules. Did you follow her into the cancer care center to make sure she went in?"

"Yes, I did, and I saw her go in there."

"But don't you believe her? Why is that?"

"Because I suspect she's pretending to be sick to manipulate Kirk into giving her money and get his attention. What if I'm making it up and I'm losing it? But I saw her shave her head before she put on a wig. Hair falls out naturally for people going through chemo. They don't have to shave their heads to be bald."

Jacklyn pats my shoulder. "Listen to your gut instincts. Maybe you can find a way to figure out what she's doing."

Irena says, "My mom had cancer and got chemotherapy, and before her hair fell out, she had me give her a buzz cut. That way, it was less upsetting when she went bald, instead of clumps of hair clogging the drain and hairbrush."

I say, "They must be powerful drugs to make your hair fall out."

Irena steers and nods. "Your fingers and toes hurt for some people, with peripheral neuropathy, like my mom got. And they can make you throw up and have diarrhea. But they also can save your life and kill the cancer cells."

Jacklyn knocks on wood. "Let's all stay healthy."

"I will," I say, "as long as I don't let this situation with Zoila get to me."

Kelly points ahead. "Look, there's Grand Island. We're almost there."

Irena says, "Prepare to dock, first mate."

Kelly grins. "I'm on it."

Jacklyn stretches. "I'll help. I miss having my own boat. Maybe I'll use Dusty's boat while he's in Shore Lodge. I'm paying for his moorage, in case he recovers, so I might as well take it out."

Irena says, "How is Dusty doing?"

Jacklyn sighs. "Not much improvement yet. But Nurse Wright says it's early days and not to get our hopes up too high. He might come through."

I frown. "After what he did to you, with his home invasion, I wouldn't blame you if you wished him dead or kept him permanently at Shore Lodge."

Jacklyn moves toward the wheelhouse door. "I

wouldn't wish ill on him because he's my flesh and blood. But he will have to stop threatening me if he recovers."

Irena says, "One can hope. He'd need a personality transplant for that."

Jacklyn opens the door, and salt air blows in. She says, "I hope he'll turn his life around, but I know the chances are small."

She steps out into the wind, gazing at the dock on Grand Island. She springs to action, says something to Kelly and drops a fender in the water. I'm in good hands on this boat, but I need to untangle the mess with Kirk when I set foot at home.

37

DUSTY

I'm parked in the dayroom, slumped over in a wheelchair. My limbs are stiff. It hurts to take a deep breath. Nurse Wright says my lungs are shot from when I was buried by the avalanche, and my lung cells might not recover. I wish the rescuers had left me for dead, instead of digging me out.

An aide comes up to me with a plastic cup. She holds a straw up to my mouth, and I wrap my lips around it, swallowing sweet apple juice. What I'd give for a beer right now, but instead I'm drinking juice and milk, like a child, and doing rehabilitation exercises, trying to lift my legs and arms.

A physical therapist about my age, in his early thirties, pushes a walker used by old folks. He stops in front of me and says, "I want you to try using the walker today. Stand up and hold onto this for one minute. Let's see how you do."

Using all my strength, I stand on wobbling, weak legs. The physical therapist counts the seconds out loud, and when he hits thirty, I drop back down in the chair, wiping my brow. I've got a long ways to go, and I don't know if I can do it. I wish I was dead.

38

JACKLYN

Irena pulls the boat up to the dock, and Kelly and I hop down, wrapping our lines around cleats. Irena turns off the engine, and Kelly jumps in place, waving her hands. "Come on, let's go. I want to see my room."

We stride up a paved road to Tex's home overlooking the water, and I say to Irena and Jenna, "I'm going to bury Albert's ashes and plant a tree on Saturday, if you'd like to come. No obligation, but just letting you know you'd be welcome. It will have been a year since he passed away that fateful day, on our wedding anniversary."

Irena reaches out and holds my hand. "Thanks, I'll be there."

Kelly says, "I wish I could but I'm staying here this weekend, to get used to being on the island."

"I'll be there," Jenna says. "What kind of tree will you plant?"

"Maybe a Leland cypress, because they bend with the wind and grow tall." An idea flashes through my head, and I let go of Irena's hand, holding up an index finger. "Come to think of it, Albert loved peonies. Pink peonies were his favorite, so I think I'll plant one of those. He'd like that."

I smile. "Maybe we should make it more of a celebration of the years we were married and make it a fun time, if we can."

Jenna glances over. "Make the best of a bad situation. I could learn from that."

Irena lugs a rolling suitcase. She nudges me and gestures to Kelly, who pulls a rolling suitcase ahead, out of earshot. "Not sure it's possible for her, given what she went through. When your grandfather betrays you, there's no silver lining. It was utterly heartbreaking. I don't think we'll ever entirely put it behind us."

I nod. "She's strong, and she'll survive and live to tell the tale and maybe help other survivors."

Irena says, "I'll catch up with Kelly. This is a big day, and I don't want her going in by herself."

Kelly strides toward the front door, and Irena hustles to catch up, hauling a suitcase. The door opens, and Tex waves to us, before Kelly and Irena head inside.

I say to Jenna, "It's just us chickens bringing up the

rear. No need for us to rush. Let's take a moment and appreciate the view before joining the others."

"Sure."

Jenna and I stand side by side by a pond, facing the Salish Sea. I rest my hands on my hips. "If you ever need legal advice, my friend Fred could help you."

"Thanks, I just saw his wife Mary this morning. She notarized a quit claim deed that Kirk signed. I had him do that, so I can keep my house, no matter what happens."

I blow out a breath. "I hope when you get home your bank accounts are intact. My husband gave away money without telling me, so I know about that first-hand and the shock it brings if you discover it. He didn't exactly tell me lies, but his omissions meant he wasn't telling the truth, and I didn't discover it until too late. By then, both he and the money were gone. He created an entitled son who expects handouts, and I should've been suspicious, but I trusted Albert completely."

"Do you regret that?"

"I do. But I had no reason to distrust him, and after he died, it was too late to scold him. I tried yelling at the ashes that are left, but it did no good. He couldn't hear me, and there was no repairing the damage that Albert did as a father by handing out money to our grown son like bags of potato chips."

Touching her elbow, I say, "But you have time to turn your boat around before you hit the rocks and run aground, as Irena might say. I hope for your sake it's not too late."

She nods. "Me too."

I take a chance and offer her a suggestion. "Perhaps you don't need to prove Zoila is faking her illness, or go to great lengths to expose her. That's a side issue, isn't it?"

Jenna cocks her head. "But if Kirk is paying for her medical treatments, as I suspect, and she isn't getting medical treatments, she's telling lies and stealing our money with a fake story. Her aim might be to get back at us for how Kirk left her for me. I'm thinking of following her into the infusion center, where chemo patients sit in recliners."

I gulp. "I don't think it sounds like a good idea. Maybe you should reconsider that."

"They might not let me in there, but I'll give it a try."

I press my lips together and keep quiet about my doubts. You can't go marching into a patient treatment area without people in charge stopping you in your tracks. Jenna is obsessed with Zoila, in a different way than her husband is, and she's determined to make the ex out to be a terrible person.

I give a last look at the water and shrug. Who am I to judge? I dislike Zoila's attitude, and I'd applaud and put on a party if she moved away. Good riddance to you in the blue velvet robe and flimsy white negligee worn on the front lawn. Don't let the door slap you on the backside on your way out of town.

We go inside, and Jenna takes in the blazing fire in the fireplace, elegant furniture and gleaming wood floors. I say, "I could move in here in a minute."

Tex comes out and gives me a hug, shaking hands with Jenna. "Welcome, I'm glad you're here. The fog has cleared, and it's going to be another beautiful day in paradise. Kelly is in her room settling in. Can I get you anything?"

"Thanks," I say. "I'd love a cup of coffee."

Tex smiles, exposing perfect white teeth. "And you, Jenna?"

"Just water, thanks. What a lovely home you have, and the view is incredible. I wouldn't get anything done working from home if I've lived here."

Tex strides into the kitchen, and we follow in her wake. "Some days, it's difficult to read a book or talk to clients, with so much going on out on the water. I go into town for groceries and doctor's appointments, but my entertainment is watching what's happening right here in front of me."

Kelly comes out and says, "Want to see my room?"

"Sure," I say, "let's go check it out. You're one lucky dog to be able to live here, my dear."

Kelly smiles. "I am."

39

ZOILA

I scoop up a last armload of clothes hanging in a bedroom closet in the house I'm renting, and Kirk tromps upstairs, wiping his brow and avoiding meeting my gaze. His shoulders sag, and he looks out the window, staring at clouds scudding past.

I hold out the clothes to him and do my best to look tired. He doesn't take the clothes, so I set them on the bed. "Hey, you're back. Will you carry these dresses over to your house and put them in my bedroom? I'm wiped out. Moving is really taking it out of me."

He shakes his head and moves away, sitting on the edge of the bed. "I can't do this anymore, Zee, I've got to protect my marriage. You can't move in with us. I'm sorry, but you just can't."

I freeze in place, and a chill sweeps up my spine. I can't

allow this to happen. I sit next to him, resting a hand on his thigh, but he scoots out of my reach. I say in a low voice, "This is because of her, isn't it? The witch of a wife you've stashed next door?"

He nods and picks at the comforter, plucking at a stray thread.

"She's got to go. It's either her or me, and you'll have to pick who matters most. I hold your secrets that can't be disclosed to the public or the police, so I win."

He swallows, and his Adam's apple moves up and down, but he doesn't say a word.

I whisper, "We could take her out and dump her body in a remote place, or push her off a boat, tied up and weighted down with anchors. I know a place where we can buy anchors cheap near the marina. They'll never find her. Do you want to do that?"

His eyes grow wide. "What are you talking about? This is nuts. I'll have no part of it."

I tilt my head. "So, you're picky about the crimes you commit, huh?"

He blinks. "What do you mean?"

Arching an eyebrow, I say, "You're fine with embezzling money, but you won't push Jenna off a boat?"

He claps a hand to his mouth. "Murder is much worse than stealing money. You make me feel sick, talking about this. If I tell her, she'll call the cops on you."

I cross my arms. "We're in this together. There will be

no telling the perfect princess Jenna about our plans, if we have any hope of pulling this off."

His face flushes, and he grabs my shoulders, shaking me. Spit flies in my face when he says, "I love her and don't want to hurt her. She's my wife."

I push away, but he's strong, and I say, "You're hurting me. Stop shaking me."

He lets go and steps back, breathing hard.

In a tight voice, I say, "You don't want to hurt your wife, but you hurt me when we were married and broke my heart. If I can't move in with you to get the help I need, I'll die alone in this house from malnutrition and cancer eating at my insides."

"Cry me a river. Forget about these lies, because you're not going to get your way, no matter how much you whine. You're not moving in with us. You're staying here. We're not going to off my wife and dump her body. It won't happen. This is the last time we'll speak of it. I'm beginning to suspect there's something wrong with you, and you're sick in the head."

I jump up, scoop up the dresses and throw them in his face. A hanger hits him in the eye, and he yelps, uttering a slew of swear words. I stamp my foot. "Don't ever shake me or speak to me like that again. If you do, before you can blink, I'll call the cops, and you'll be carted away in handcuffs in the back of a squad car."

He rubs his eye, and his hand trembles.

I say, "Understood? Are we clear?"

"Yeah, I hear you loud and clear."

"Let's get back to business. You promised that I could live with you, and you'd take care of me. You can't change your mind now. It's too late."

He stomps a foot on my favorite little black dress, crumpled on the floor. "Jenna's upset, and I can't risk my marriage by helping you."

"You don't have a choice. I hold the cards and can call to report your theft from the hot tub company. You'll be packed off to prison, so long, bye, bye. So either I move in, while Jenna's on the boat, or I call the authorities. Which is it going to be?"

His gaze flits around the room. "I'm screwed either way."

I tap a toe. "Time's wasting. Make up your mind."

He tugs on an ear lobe, studying the floor.

I bend and scoop up the clothes, shoving them into his hands. "Come on, let's go. We're moving me out, so you can save money. This way, you won't pay rent. Doesn't that sound good?"

He clenches his jaw and doesn't answer.

I study his weak chin with sparse stubble and wonder what I ever saw in him. He's a mere means to an end. But no matter what I do, it'll never heal the wounds he made by leaving me for another woman.

I point to a suitcase I packed earlier. "Come on, let's go. We don't have much left to move, so it won't take long. If you take the suitcase on this trip, I'll take some of these dresses."

He grabs the suitcase and clomps down the stairs. "You have a lot of clothes."

I glance at his sullen face and let a dress fall from my hands. "Oh, drat. Can you pick that up for me? I can't reach it with my hands full."

He does as I requested, and I reward him with a smile. Little by little, I'm training him to follow my orders and not ask questions. With a giggle, I say, "A girl's got to have clothes."

Going next door, we climb the stairs to my new bedroom facing the back garden. I curl up in bed with my head on a pillow.

He sets the suitcase down on the floor. "What's in this anyway? It's heavy."

"My many negligees and ten-pound weights."

He shrugs. "You don't look like you're lifting weights much these days."

"I'm not. But if you act nice, I might show you the new black negligee I bought the other day with you in mind."

He clears his throat, clenches his jaw and looks away.

Letting out a weary sigh, I stretch my arms. "I'm exhausted. Can you clear out the other stuff while I take a nap? The doctor told me to rest when I'm tired. By the way, I like where this bedroom is, right next to yours."

He shakes his head and moves to the doorway.

I smile. "This will be fun, us living together again. I'll spoil you with lots of attention. You'll love it."

The door downstairs swings open, and Jenna calls, "Anyone home?"

Kirk's eyes open wide, and he visibly tenses, turning and walking out of the bedroom. He calls, "Up here, hon. How was your boat trip?"

40

IRENA

Docking in my home slip in the marina in Millersville, I check my dock lines. Jacklyn and Jenna walk away, and I blow my nose. Kelly usually helps me scrub down the boat after I dock. I miss her already.

Before getting out a bucket and brush to scrub salt water off the boat, I call Kelly's father to tell him what happened on Grand Island.

Jack picks up and says, "How did it go? Are you back in town?"

"Yeah, I'm in Millersville, and Kelly is beyond happy. I met the teacher for the one-room schoolhouse, and she was great, with lots of energy and a warm person, and Kelly liked her. I'm happy for her, but I feel like we've lost our little girl."

"I hope this'll be good and give her a break from kids gossiping and spreading nasty lies about her."

"I hope so. It was tough, leaving her to live with someone else. She'll spend this week and the weekend there to get used to it. Next weekend, she'll come home. I'll go get her, and you can see her."

He says in a soft voice, "I already miss her. I wish we could go in your boat to see her."

"Are you and Abby well enough for a trip like that?"

"Not yet. It'll be our stretch goal to aim for."

"Do you guys need food? I'm doing a grocery run. It's not like there's anything else to do."

"No, we're set for a while, thanks. You inherited Buzz's house, is that right?"

I let out a sigh. "I did."

"What are you going to do with it, if you know?"

My eyebrows shoot up, and I wonder if he's angling for me to give it to him, because Buzz caused the head injury that wiped out much of Jack's memory. "I'm not sure, but it doesn't seem right to sell it."

"Maybe keep the house for Kelly to have when she finishes high school or college. That might lure her back, instead of moving to Seattle, like she's talked about. Maybe by then she'll see there's a lot to be said for living in a small town like Millersville."

I smile. "There is, and the best part is having people like you and Abby close by. Okay if I come get the dog in a bit?"

"Sure, we liked having him, but he needs a walk, and we're not up for that yet."

We hang up, and I give the boat a quick wash before heading out to get the dog Buzz left behind. I park in front of Jack and Abby's place, hurry up the front walk and knock on the door.

"Coming," Jack calls. The dog whines inside, scratching the door.

I bend and say to the dog named Happy on the other side of the door, "Hang on. You're going home with me."

Happy lets out a high-pitched yip and barks. When Jack opens the door, the dog bounds out, rubbing against my leg, and I bend to pet him. Looking up at Jack with a smile, I say, "Thanks, I'd better get going."

"See you later, and thanks for being such a good mom to Kelly."

I nod and take Happy down the block to do his business before we get in the car. Driving away, I break into a wide smile, recalling Jack's words, which I've always wanted to hear him say. When we were married, I felt like I was doing everything alone, but now three of us are raising Kelly. It's a relief to have friends like Abby and Jack backing me up and taking my side in parenting.

I lower the rear windows a few inches, and Happy sits in the back seat, sniffing the air. "That's right, we're heading to your old house, and you'll run in the fenced yard. We're almost there." Happy lifts his nose to the window and barks.

Driving to the house Buzz owned, I grip the steering wheel and hope what I'll find in the closet won't be creepy but just a pleasant reminder of my dear long-time lost friend.

41

JENNA

When Jacklyn drops me off, I open the front door to my house and sniff the air, detecting Zoila's perfume in my home.

I call, "Anyone home?"

"Up here," Kirk says, tromping down the stairs. His lips form a thin line, and he won't meet my eyes. "How was your boat trip?"

I cock my head. "What's going on? You look upset."

He points upstairs and says in a low voice, "I'm sorry, but she insisted on moving in with us. I couldn't stop her."

I wrinkle my nose, observing how timid he is around Zoila. But this is my home, and I won't abandon it. If Kirk can't stand up to Zoila, they both have to leave.

Zoila comes to the top of the stairs, wearing a white nightgown and a blue floor length velvet robe. Her face is pale, although from here it looks like she used powder, and she says in a weak voice, "I'm not feeling well. I'll be in my room taking a nap, and I might go to sleep early tonight. I'm worn out from the stress of moving. It was a lot of work." She gives him a sly smile.

I clench my jaw, resisting the urge to roll my eyes. She is truly over the top. I can't believe Kirk hasn't seen through her act.

She shuffles away, and I take Kirk aside, whispering, "What were you thinking, letting her move in here? I won't have it. She's got to go when she wakes up from her nap, or you both have to leave."

Zoila's voice wafts down the stairs. "I can hear you. Don't be upset with me, Jenna. I just need a place to crash."

My heart races, and I turn to Kirk. "You have twenty-four hours to get her out. If you don't, I'll kick you both out and call the police if I have to. This is my home."

I storm to my office, and Kirk trots behind me. "Wait. Let's talk this out."

Stepping into my office, I say, "No amount of talking will fix this, and you've lost your perspective. I won't have her in my house, and that's final."

I close and lock my office door, but he rattles the knob. "Let me in."

I put on a pair of headphones to drown out the madness and open my laptop, going online and checking our bank accounts. My hands turn cold, and I stare at the screen. He moved money in a series of transfers. He also wrote checks to Zoila for thousands of dollars.

Sitting back in my swivel chair, I drum my fingers on the desk and mull over my options. I didn't want to consider divorce, but I've got to get out of this downward spiral. Kirk is taking me down with him. I'll boot them out of my house and file for divorce. Kirk can fawn on his ex-wife somewhere else.

I lean forward in the chair and click to open a new bank account, entering my name and transferring what money we have left from our joint account to my new one. I must protect what's mine before Zoila drains all our money.

Tilting my head, I consider a question running through my mind. What hold does she have over him that gives her so much power, because he jumps at her every request? I suspect it's due to something other than her sex appeal, but I won't hang around long enough to find out what it is. She has a tight hold on him that he can't shake.

42

IRENA

I open the front door of the house I inherited and step inside, inhaling musty air. Happy bounds in, barking and running from room to room, probably searching for Buzz. I blink back tears because he left the planet too soon when he jumped off Jackson Bridge. Wood floor boards creak under my feet. The closed-up space smells of dust, old books and something rotting.

I let the dog out into the fenced back yard and go to the refrigerator, glancing at a magnet with a photo of Kelly and me. Biting my lip and missing her, I open the fridge door and look inside. Gray furry mold greets me, giving off an overwhelming stench. I gag and close the fridge door.

A horrible odor wafts from around the sink. Opening cupboard doors below the sink, I gasp, seeing a dead rat.

Slamming the cupboards shut, I shudder and march into the living room.

Opening my arms, I say, "Thanks for the house, Buzz, but there's moldy food in the fridge and a dead rat to deal with. I'm not exactly complaining about your gift, but I guess I am. If you hadn't lied about hurting Jack, you might still be alive."

Putting my hands on my hips, I study stacks of books on the floor, book shelves and the coffee table. To say he loved books is an understatement. "I'm not sure what to do with your gift, but thanks. I'll clean up this place in my spare time."

Drawn to the second bedroom, I tiptoe to the locked closet door, slip in the key and open it. Before me is what looks like a shrine to someone he loved, with votive candles, a white leatherbound book and a silver-framed photo taken in grade school of me, with a goofy smile on my face.

I pick up the leather notebook and read a few lines, leafing through pages. I recognize his flowing cursive writing, and my eyebrows shoot up when I realize he wrote a series of love poems, with me as the subject of his ardor. Gently setting the book of poems down, I close the closet door, lock it and lean against it, holding back the past and barricading the passions held within. I'll read the poems another time. Right now, I've got a dead rat to contend with and a refrigerator to clean.

43

KIRK

Opening my laptop in my office, I go online to transfer more money to Zoila's bank account, but when I log in, my fingers freeze, and I stare at the screen. The bank balance is much lower than when I checked yesterday. There's barely enough for me to pay the household bills and get coffee with Zoila before dropping her off at the cancer center.

I jump up and hurry to my wife's study door, turning the knob, but it is locked. Knocking on it, I say, "Hon, what happened to the money we had in the bank? It disappeared."

She doesn't answer, so I say, "I know you're in there. You've got to speak to me at some point and tell me what you did."

I hear her speaking in low tones on the phone, setting

up an appointment. Clearing my throat, I say, "Who are you talking to? What's going on?"

"Nothing you need concern yourself with," she says through the door. "Go take care of Zoila. I'm sure she needs your help."

Zoila calls out from upstairs. "Kirk, I need you. Can you come help me with something?"

I stare at the closed door and mutter, "Whatever."

I run upstairs to do my former wife's bidding. All I have to do is stop Zoila from reporting what she knows. Then maybe I'll take a page from her book and send her down to the bottom of the sea, wrapped with ropes, with anchors around her neck. She's pure evil, so it might take more than two anchors to do the job. She doesn't give up easily.

Climbing the final step on the stairs, I enter Zoila's bedroom, where she is on the bed wearing very little and wiggling her slender fingers at me. Without a word, I pivot and stride down the stairs to save myself and my marriage, but I have a feeling it's too late for that. It's my fault, and I've been duplicitous. My misdeeds are biting me in the backside, and there's little chance of escaping my past.

44

IRENA

I lean into the fridge and scrub with a sponge until the surface shines. I threw out green moldy cheese, a container of furry sour cream and everything else in the fridge. Breathing through my mouth and bending down under the sink, I scooped up a stinking dead rat with a garden trowel and dumped the stiff body in a garbage bag, dropping it in a trash can outside. Happy ran over and barked, but I shook my head. "Not for you, sweet boy."

Inhaling fresh air, I wipe my brow with the back of my hand. My phone rings, and I stab at my phone, accepting a video call from my daughter.

"Hey, sweetie."

"Hi, Mom."

"How are you?"

She beams. "Great. I love it here. I'm glad you and Dad let me try it out."

I bite my lower lip and wish I was with her, but she's on an island far from town. I say, "How's school?"

"The teacher's really nice."

"Have you met any kids yet?"

"Tex and I walked to the store. She bought me a chocolate chip cookie, and she got an oatmeal one, and we sat outside eating them. A boy my age came by on his bike and talked to us."

My pulse picks up. I wipe a frown off my face and remind myself it will be a long time before Kelly falls for a boy. "Oh? What's he like?"

Her cheeks flush. "He rides a dirt bike, and he invited me to go with him."

My eyebrows shoot up, and I say, "Absolutely not, no way are you getting on a dirt bike and racing around. It's too dangerous."

"That's what Tex said too. No dirt biking until I'm older."

I nod. "You have to be at least eighteen to do that."

She rolls her eyes. "Come on, Mom. I can't wait that long. Besides, everyone on the island is doing it."

I tilt my head. "If they asked you to jump off a cliff, would you?"

"Can we not do this?"

With a sigh, I chastise myself for alienating my

daughter in a short amount of time, and I change the subject. "What are you guys having for dinner?"

"We're going to a neighbor's house for dinner." She wrinkles her nose and says in a low voice, "We're having venison stew. What if I don't like it?"

"You know what to do. Take a few bites and say something nice about it. You don't have to finish it, just be polite. Be discreet."

She nods. "I'll do that. Oh, here's Tex, she wants to talk to you."

"Wait," I say, "what's the name of this boy on the dirt bike?"

But it's too late, and Tex is on the phone, smiling at me and flashing her perfect white teeth. "Hey, Irena, how are you holding up without Kelly there?"

"I'm cleaning. I was deep into Buzz's smelly fridge, and I took a dead rat out to the trash."

"Sounds like fun, sorry we're missing it," she says sarcastically.

I give her a half-smile. "I'm living large, all on my own. How's it going there?"

Tex says, "Everything is fine. Kelly's doing great."

"I'm glad to hear it. Thank you for having her. We really appreciate it. Jack and Abby want to come over to visit when they get better, and I'll come over in a few days to pop in for an hour or so."

A flicker of a frown crosses Tex's face. "Do you think

that's wise? I thought she might need more time than that to acclimate before seeing you. It might make her homesick and confuse her if it's too soon. But whatever you think is best. You're her mother."

We say goodbye, and I hang up. I massage my temples, where a headache throbs. I've got to work on not blurting out the first thing that comes to mind with my daughter, or I'll destroy all trust between us.

The dog yips and barks out back, and I stride over to see what's bothering him. A large tabby cat sits on top of a new small structure in the yard. Buzz must have built it before he died, and the building looks like a tiny church with space inside for one person.

The cat jumps onto a fence and disappears into the next yard. The dog whines and whimpers, leaning against my leg and looking up at me. I rub his ears and pat his back. "I know, we both miss Buzz, but he's not coming back. I'm sorry, pup. But it'll get better with time."

Something about the tiny building beckons, and I step over to it, opening the door and inhaling the smell of cedar lumber. I settle on a small handwoven rug in the middle of the structure. Crossing my legs, I look around. A sign in front of me burned into wood says, 'Be a Better Person.'

I nod. "That's spot on and a good reminder, my friend. That night when you left Jack must've really bothered you, which it should've."

The dog barges into the tiny building, sitting by me panting. I pat his back. "It's just us now. And he's right, I need to be a better person. But you, you're perfect, just the way you are."

The dog licks my face, and I laugh.

45

JENNA

The next morning, I meet with Jacklyn's friend Fred, who is an attorney, in his office downtown. He looks over the top of his glasses. "Are you sure you want to do this? It's a big step, and not one takes lightly."

I whoosh out a breath and lean forward in a chair facing the desk. "I'm sure. My husband moved his ex-wife into our home, and he's giving her money, but not telling me about it. They're close and acting like they're still married, and I'm the odd one out. They can have a life together, if they want, but not with me in it. I want nothing to do with him anymore."

"Fine, you sound quite sure of your decision, so I'll go ahead and prepare the paperwork. I'll give you a call when you can come pick it up, and you can serve the papers to him. Now, about our fee. How will you be paying? Check, credit card or Zaybo?"

My hands are cold and moist. My heart thuds. I never thought this day would come, but my life has been turned upside down. If I don't divorce Kirk, I don't think I'll survive.

I say, "I'll put it on the joint credit card, so he can see the consequences of his actions."

He cocks his head. "You might want the element of surprise to avoid an unpleasant confrontation. But it's your choice, of course."

We shake hands and say goodbye, and I hurry to my car. Tears run down my cheeks, and I lean over the steering wheel, sobbing and grieving for what we've lost. With Zoila in the picture and ever-present, the life I envisioned with Kirk has evaporated.

Driving home, I stop in a drive-through for coffee, and my hands tremble as I take the cup. I left the house in a hurry this morning and didn't brew a pot of coffee like I usually do. I didn't want to deal with Kirk, who has become a wet noodle. It's blatantly obvious where his loyalties lie.

I put the coffee in a cup holder and drive home, patting my roiling stomach and grimacing at the thought of my nemesis waiting at home, marring my beautiful guest bedroom facing the back garden. That lovely space was never intended to be occupied by her. The battle lines are drawn, and they must move.

When I walk in the door, Kirk appears, waving his hands. His hair stands on end, and he's wearing a blue terrycloth bathrobe I gave him for his birthday. He frowns. "Where have you been? You walked out and didn't tell me where you were going. I couldn't find you in the house, and you didn't answer your phone or my texts."

I shrug. "I went for a ride to clear my head. Is Zoila up yet? I came back to take her to the cancer care center for her chemo infusion."

His face goes blank. "Oh, okay, I'll go get her."

Zoila sweeps into the kitchen, wearing my long flower-print dress Kirk bought me for our first anniversary that was hanging in my closet. He nods to her, and my chest tightens at his betrayal.

She giggles. "I couldn't figure out what to wear, so Kirk picked this out from your clothes. I hope you don't mind if I borrow it for a little bit?"

I shrug, because it doesn't matter if she wears my clothes. My heart is hardening more with each moment spent in their presence, and I've reached the point where she can have my husband. He took my money. He gave her my dress. He responds to her every request. It's so bad now, it can't possibly get worse.

She smiles. "I'm ready."

I grin, plotting my revenge. "Then let's go."

46

———

JACKLYN

ooking out my front window, I happen to see Jenna drive by with Zoila. I shake my head and say to Mercury, who is over having coffee, "What's going on at Jenna's place is getting stranger and stranger. I just saw her go by with Kirk's ex-wife in the car. I wonder where they're going?"

Mercury grunts and drinks coffee from his perch on the living room couch. "Don't stick your nose in it. You might get blamed for stirring things up. That never works out."

I sit in an armchair and lean back, taking a sip of strong black coffee. "I hear you, but I can't help but be curious. You wouldn't believe what Jenna has to put up with, living with Kirk's ex-wife. He moved her in, can you believe it? And you should see how Zoila slinks around. I think she's a master manipulator, but Kirk doesn't see it that way at all."

"Keep your nose out of it."

Buddy scratches at the back door, and I get up to let him in. Cold wind races down the street, and tree branches sway back and forth, doing a winter dance. I shiver, pulling my fleece jacket close, and Buddy runs inside. He laps up water from a bowl, trots over to Mercury and hops up next to him on the sofa. Mercury reaches out and scratches behind my dog's ears, and I sit and smile at them.

Mercury says, "Do you want to go to your old garden store and pick up a plant for your ceremony on Saturday?"

I nod. "I do. I didn't get around to it yesterday. I've been thinking it'll be odd to show up there, in a place I owned, before my son sold it out from under me. I loved running that store. The routine of going to work helped when I was grieving Albert's death and kept me on track. But now I'll have to find a new meaning and purpose, because I'm not going to build big homes. My husband always said life is like a river, with twists and turns, and we don't know where it will take us."

Mercury tugs on his gray mustache. "He sounds like a wise man. Wish I'd met him."

"You would've liked him, and the two of you would've gotten along well. If you're willing to go with me, let's take Buddy for a walk and then stop in at Werner's for a pink peony. I didn't have time to do that until now."

We sit in silence for a moment, mulling things over. He tips his cup back, swallows a slug of coffee and sets the cup down on a side table. "You mentioned you're thinking of having a retreat center with classes on your property? Isn't that kind of thing already offered in other places around town?"

I purse my lips and nod. My idea for my next step is fluid and being formed, and I'm flexible about what shape it will take. "It was a good idea in the night, but you're right, other places offer classes. It would cost a fair amount to build, burning up cash, and I'd have to hire someone to run it, because I don't want to manage it. So, maybe a retreat center isn't such a good idea after all. I'll table it for now."

He pats Buddy's head, and I sit forward, saying, "But tiny homes are a great idea and will fill a need in the community. People will be able to afford to buy them. It'll be less of a financial burden to build them. I definitely want to do that and create a big fenced dog park. What do you think of that?"

He smiles. "Sounds reasonable and attainable and financially sustainable. I wonder if you might want an investor or two to go in on the project, for input and to lower your risk?"

"I'll think about it. Do you have anyone in mind?"

"If Irena inherited Buzz's investment accounts, she might be interested."

"I thought you were going to suggest I ask Tex."

Buddy noses his arm, rolling over on his back, and Mercury pats his belly. "No, I wouldn't impose on Tex that way. From what I hear, she's got her hands full with Irena's business as part-owner, her other projects and overseeing Kelly on the island. She's got a lot going on."

"She does, but asking Irena to come in on the project is a good idea. She's someone I could work with. I'll drop the name Stone Estates, which Dusty and his dad picked, and come up with a new concept."

"How about something like Tiny Homes with a View? Or Viewlands?"

I slap my knee and stand, and Buddy looks over. "I like that. It fits the setting and is different from what my son planned. It'll be a fresh start for the parcel of land and me, so it's perfect. But I'll see what Irena says about View-lands, if she becomes an investor."

47

ZOILA

Jenna drives to the cancer center and hums to herself, keeping her eyes on the road. I watch her carefully, because something has changed in her demeanor. She's not nosy or asking me questions, or trying to find holes in my story about being sick. Yesterday, at my birthday dinner, she acted like a victim. Now, she has energy and a fresh resolve, and I don't like what I'm seeing. I want her to feel downtrodden, alone and as helpless as I did when Kirk left me.

"You're acting different," I say, squinting at her. "You're upbeat, like you don't have a care in the world."

She shrugs. "I wish, but let's just say I'm taking matters into my own hands."

I push my fingernail into my palm and grimace. "What does that mean?"

She tips her head back and laughs. "It's too soon to say, but you'll find out."

I frown and turn to stare out the side window, watching life flash past. A sinking feeling comes over me, which is new, because I almost always get my way, except for with Jacklyn the neighbor who thwarted me. She led neighbors to gang up against me, but all I did was feed poor, helpless creatures. So what if there were more and more raccoons gathering in the neighbors' yards?

Jenna pulls over and parks a block from the chemo center. She starts to get out, but I tap her arm. "I can't walk that far. Can you drop me off and pick me up?"

"Oh, gosh, sorry, my mistake. I apologize. I'll find something closer. Hold on."

She starts the car and drives to the cancer care center, this time pulling into a spot near the entrance. I hop out and wave to her. "See you later. Thanks for the ride. I'll text you when I'm finished with treatment."

She climbs out of the car and slams the door shut. "I'll come with you."

I wave a hand in front of my face. "No need. I'm all set."

"Fine," she says, slowing down and stopping to look at her phone.

I rush in through the sliding glass doors and hurry up the steps to the second floor. I might as well get some much-needed exercise, since she isn't looking. I glance back and spot her planted in the same place outside and breathe a sigh of relief. I'm safe from her prying eyes for the time being.

I slowly walk up to the check in counter, take a visitor's badge and pin it to my dress. Looking down, I smile, admiring Jenna's black leather boots I borrowed. They won't know what hit them in a week. I'll be Hurricane Zoila, wreaking havoc in my wake.

Pulling open a door, I enter the cancer care infusion center and mosey past pale, thin patients dozing in recliners. IV poles hold plastic bags of medications, dripping into their systems and bringing health to some by killing cancer cells.

I nod to a nurse and pretend I belong here as a family member or volunteer like I always do. Slipping out a side door, I stride to a bathroom and go inside, stopping at the sinks. The door opens behind me and closes with a thud.

Jenna crosses her arms. "I knew you were faking it, and this proves it. You're scamming my husband just to get money, aren't you?"

Clapping a hand to my chest, I think fast and cook up an excuse. "You don't understand. The nurse told me to come back in a half hour. They're backed up and can't take me yet."

She taps a toe. "That's nonsense. You've been lying to us. Drop the act."

My pulse races, and I march up to her, intending to intimate her. It works on Kirk and everyone else. Poking a finger in her face, I say, "It's none of your business whether I have cancer or not, and you have no idea what's going on. My type of cancer doesn't require chemo every time, and today I'm actually going for tests to see if my heart is okay, because some treatments damage the heart. But you wouldn't know that, would you, miss know-it-all, so give me a break. Go home, and I'll see you there. I'll catch a ride another way. I don't need you sticking your nose into my business."

I fling open the door and hurry out of the bathroom, but she marches after me, saying, "Zoila, stop. We need to talk."

I turn to look back, and her jaw tenses. Before I can react, she strides over, reaches out and snatches off my wig. Cool air drifts over my bare scalp. I wave a hand in the air and lunge for my wig, but she steps away.

"Give it back," I say in a loud voice and hope someone will come to my aid.

She grins, "I knew it. Your hair hasn't fallen out. I saw you shaving your head. This proves you're faking being sick. You don't have cancer. You're a liar and a thief."

A stout security guard storms toward us, glowering, and I whimper and cower, holding my hands over my head. In a loud voice, I say, "How can you be so mean to me? I'm a patient getting care in this facility. Help."

The guard strides over to us, and she points toward the door, telling Jenna, "You must leave this facility. We have zero-tolerance for people harassing our patients."

Jenna says, "But, she's taking our money, and she isn't sick. She's stealing, and that's a crime."

The guard frowns. "You'll be trespassed if you don't leave right away. Let's go. I'll usher you out. And give her back her wig. You should be ashamed of yourself for taking it. That's just nasty and mean-spirited, if you ask me."

Jenna cringes and tosses me the wig. I catch it and put it on my head, pulling it down. I say to her. "Run home to your husband."

She scowls. "Just you wait."

The guard takes her by the arm, hustles her down the steps and out the door.

When she looks back, I wave goodbye and smile. She walks away, and I whistle a happy tune and head for the coffee stand, where I order a tall caramel latte with extra foam on top. I'm spending Kirk's money and treating myself, enjoying the ride for however long it lasts.

48

JACKLYN

I stand and say, "Ready for our walk? Then I'll buy a pink peony." Mercury gets off the sofa and picks up his coffee cup. "Sure." Buddy hops off the couch, shaking in place, metal tags clanging.

Mercury says, "Not the best day for it, but we might as well get some exercise."

Departing the warm house, we march around in the wind, and Buddy's ears blow back. Three deer nibble on grass, and we pass on by. No need to ogle them when our town has tame deer living in the forest lands and on trimmed lawns. Even Buddy does a dog shrug when he sees the deer, because they're a common sight.

Forty minutes later, we drop Buddy off at home and hop in the car, heading to the garden store I owned until Dusty took a wrecking ball to my life. Mercury drives, and I say, "I'm nervous about this. What if I see Carolyn, the new owner? I wish I still owned the store, and I don't want to break down in tears."

"However you react will be fine. We'll buy a bush to plant with your husband's ashes, and that's all this errand is about. It doesn't have to be about dredging up the past."

I drum my fingers on the seat. "But it is about confronting my past, and I can't ignore my feelings. It was my home away from home, and I haven't been back since Dusty sold the store."

He nods. "I see why you're nervous. Your store holds a lot of meaning for you. But I'll be by your side, supporting you."

I reach over and pat his arm as he parks outside the store that was mine a year ago. I open the car door and step outside, and Mercury joins me on the sidewalk.

I say, "Okay, our plan is to buy a peony and vamoose back home to the best dog in the world. We won't linger long."

Mercury chuckles. "He's a good dog, I'll give you that."

Inside, the store looks the same, and rubber plants occupy the same corner of the shop. No one is at the check-out counter as we breeze by, thank goodness, so I don't have to go through the process of idle chit chat, pretending I'm happy I don't own the business.

Going out to a fenced nursery area, I point to where the peonies used to be and purse my lips, seeing an empty spot. "The peonies were there. I hope they're not out of stock, or they stopped carrying them. If they are, I'll have to drive to the valley to get one."

Carolyn, the new owner, strides over, smiling and fairly vibrating with energy. "Jacklyn, you came back." She throws her arms open and gives me a hug.

Embracing her, I smell coffee on her breath and a hint of lavender wafting off her denim work shirt. Stepping away, I say, "Are you out of peonies? I hope not, because I'm here to buy one to plant with Albert's ashes in my yard. Oh, and this is my friend Mercury. Mercury, this is Carolyn."

He shakes her hand. "Nice to meet you."

She tilts her head. "Are you local?"

"Yep, I live here."

"I haven't seen you around."

He adjusts a red polka dot bow tie affixed to his long gray beard. "I mostly keep to myself. I make violins and give lessons."

Carolyn beams. "Well, Jacklyn is one of my favorite people, and I'm honored to own this store. I was so excited to buy it when you decided to sell it."

I say, "I didn't want to sell it. Dusty went ahead without my permission."

Carolyn crosses her arms. "I'm so sorry it happened that way, but I hope you don't want it back. I've always wanted to own this store from the first day I set foot in it. The place feels like home."

She gestures to the twinkling fairy lights in the eaves

and running along the fence, and I wipe a tear from my eye. "It felt like home to me too, but no, I don't want it back. That's water under the bridge, and I'm moving on. I'm thinking of building tiny homes on a parcel of land above town."

Her eyes open wide. "That's a great idea. Everyone will want one. Homes are too expensive in this area now, so I'm sure it'll be a huge success. I might want to buy one."

I smile. "That's good to know. I'll keep you in mind. Now about the peony, do you happen to have a pink peony in stock? I'd like a pretty one to plant on Saturday."

"We moved them over there. Come with me."

We follow Carolyn to a new outdoor area, where five perfect peonies await new soil to flourish and blossom. I sigh, recalling how Albert loved when I'd clip peony blossoms, float them in a bowl of water and set it on the dining table, the very table Dusty threw out. I shake my head at how my son embraced the dark side after his dad died, deceiving me and making off with my money.

Mercury's voice brings me back to the present. "See one you like?"

I nod. One plant in particular calls to me, with many green leaves. It looks hardy, which is what I've had to be during my winter of widowhood this past year. I point and say, "I'll take that one. How much do I owe you?"

Carolyn waves her hands. "Oh, no, you won't be paying for this plant. It's our gift to say thanks for passing on your lovely store to me and allowing me to run it.

Albert would have liked this plant, so take it home, plant it and know that your store is in good hands. And that's because of the work you two put in over the years, creating goodwill in the community and building a following of loyal customers who miss you and ask about you."

My throat grows tight with tears, but I manage to say, "Thank you. I appreciate the gesture. Now, I'd better get out of here before I break down and cry like a baby. See you later."

Mercury picks up the plant, and we hurry outside, putting the bush in the back of the car, setting it sideways for the short drive home on a blue plastic tarp to protect the seats. We hop in, and while he drives, tears stream down my cheeks and mixed emotions wash over me. Grief, relief, gratefulness, along with a feeling of closure and awe at what lies ahead floods my body. I release a sigh, welcoming whatever will happen next.

I roll down the window halfway and breathe in briny sea air. We turn a corner and go down the block, and I frown, recalling how Dusty cleared out my house after he admitted me to Shore Lodge. I returned to an empty home, and he never apologized for what he did.

Mercury says, "Everything okay?"

"Yes, and getting better every day. I just have a lot of thoughts racing through my mind."

"Understood. Let me know if you want to talk anything over."

"Thanks, I will."

Rolling up my window, I glance north toward Shore Lodge. I can't see it from my home, but the stark facility is lurking there all the same, trapping my son inside. I'll be fine as long as Dusty remains locked in the second-floor unit on Cedar Island. But if he gets out, I suspect he'll go on a rampage and tear down my life all over again.

49
_____

KIRK

Jenna comes in the house and slams the door, making window panes rattle in their frames. I leave my desk and hurry into the hall. "Hon, what's going on?"

"Zoila is moving."

My pulse picks up. "We can't abandon her when she needs us. It would be cruel."

Jenna frowns. "When are you going to wake up? She wasn't getting chemo today, like she said she was. She's been telling these lies, and you're swallowing them whole."

I open my hands. "You're not getting it. She's sick, and we're helping her. It's a simple story."

She puts her hands on her hips. "You gave her money from our checking account and didn't tell me. You should've been honest with me and not gone behind my back. You've changed when Zoila came to town, and you're not the man I married."

I advance toward her, but she steps back, holding up her hands. "Don't get any closer. It's insane that you're insisting on the three of us living together. You're siding with her, and you didn't believe me when I said she doesn't have cancer. She wants our money. Your moving her into my home marks the end of us, and I'm through with you and our marriage. You and your ex can get a room at a No-Tell Motel for all I care."

I clench my hands. "You don't understand. She is forcing me to do this."

Her eyes are cold when she says, "I'm not sure what you mean by that. Just grow a backbone and stand up to her."

"Our lives would be ruined if I did."

"It's already ruined. What's going on between you two means we're over."

Zoila comes inside, dropping her purse on the floor. She points at Jenna and frowns, saying to me, "Did you hear how she accosted me at the cancer center? A security guard kicked her out for harassing me."

I whip around to stare at my wife. "Is that true?"

Jenna shakes her head. "I exposed her lies. But you're eating up every morsel she tosses out without questioning the source. When are you going to step back and see her for who she really is?"

I flinch. "Zoila's not like that. You don't know her as well as I do."

Zoila tugs on my arm. "She ripped my wig off. I was mortified. It was awful."

I turn to my wife. "Is this true? I thought I knew you, but I was wrong."

Jenna shrugs, and I lean in, watching her every move. She doesn't look upset in the least by my harsh words.

Jenna says, "The love we had died when you moved her next door. You gave her our money for cancer treatments, without talking to me. When I told you she's faking her illness and fooling you, you believed her over me. And finally, you moved her into my home over my objections. She has ulterior motives, but you don't doubt her. She's taking advantage of you, and you don't want to see it. I think that about sums it up."

Zoila leans in, gripping my arm. "I'm telling you the truth. She was cruel to me today. My bare head was exposed when she pulled off my wig. It was horrible."

I say, "I'm sorry about that."

Jenna stomps upstairs.

Zoila says, "Is she acting like that because of menopause?"

Jenna yells down from the upstairs railing. "It's not menopause. I'm fed up with you inserting yourself into every crevice of our lives. Move on and find another target to milk for money."

Clapping a hand to my chest, I step to the bottom of the stairs and tell Jenna, "That was rude."

Jenna rolls her eyes. "I'm only getting started. Zoila, stop being a leech and move out. I see you for who you really are, beneath your silky clothes and swaying hips, I know what you're up to. You want our money. And I bet you want my husband."

Jenna steps away and comes back, holding a blown glass sculpture from our master bedroom over the railing upstairs. A shiver runs up my spine. I bought that piece of art for her, and it cost me a month's salary.

"Stop," I say, "put that back. It's expensive. Jenna, think before you do something rash."

The glass sculpture comes flying down, shattering on the steps and floor, scattering glittering shards. I close my eyes and groan at the thousands of dollars gone in one final crazy impulse act.

"Stop," I call to Jenna, "enough."

But a second glass sculpture flies down the stairs, breaking on impact into bits.

In a shaking voice, I say, "What do you want? I'll give it to you, just stop."

"I want the two of you to move out of my home. Leave, now."

Zoila pouts her red full lips, whining, "I don't want to go. Do you?"

I clear my throat. "No, I want to stay and settle this."

Jenna says, "Zoila, you can go back to wherever you

came from. Move next door or move away. I just want the two of you gone."

Jenna appears at the top of the stairs brandishing a butcher knife I sharpened last week. "Get out of here, before I call the police and report you for stealing."

Zoila wrinkles her nose. "He paid me to stop me from reporting his crimes."

Jenna's mouth falls open. "What crimes, Kirk?"

I don't answer. I squeeze Zoila's hand to keep her from blurting out my secret.

Jenna says, "Kirk, what crimes is she talking about? Is she telling the truth?"

I turn to my former wife, who is an anchor around my neck. "Zoila, grab your things. We're going next door, and we don't have much time. She's losing it."

I shove my laptop in a bag and exit the house, followed by Zoila. She grumbles and says, "This isn't how I expected it to go. It was supposed to be the three of us living together while I go through treatment."

"Looks like that's not going to happen," I say, letting myself into the house I'm renting for her. This morning, I emailed the owners to say they could come back anytime. I hope they don't check their email and show up while we're hiding from Jenna's wrath.

I stumble into the living room, set my laptop bag on the floor and look next door, where Jenna is staring at us, with her arms crossed. I've made a royal mess, and there's no way out.

50

JACKLYN

On Saturday morning, I get up before dawn and shuffle to the kitchen, making a pot of coffee. I pour two scoops of kibble into Buddy's bowl, adding a bit of wet dog food from a can, and he gobbles it down. While the coffee brews, I pull on my winter jacket and leash him up, and we march around the block in heavy mist. At six in the morning, it is pitch-black. Something moves close by, and I aim my flashlight at a coyote up ahead, crossing the road and loping into a forested area.

I say in a low voice to my dog, so as not to wake sleeping neighbors, "Good thing we didn't see him face to face." As I walk, I run through plans for the peony planting today. By the time we get home, the house smells like fresh-brewed coffee in the morning, the coffee pot is full, and I'm looking forward to my peony planting ashes event.

Pouring steaming black coffee into a mug, I mull over what to say when burying the peony and shrug. I'll mark the occasion with whatever words spring to mind at the moment, speaking from the heart. No need to worry about it and get nervous.

Mercury's car pulls up, and I open the door for him. He gives me a kiss on the lips and comes inside. "Coffee?" I say, gesturing to the kitchen.

"Does a pig sit on pressed ham? That's a yes for me."

I set a cup before him at the kitchen table, and he gazes at me. "You seem pretty calm, given what you're about to do. Burying his ashes is a big step, and I'm glad you asked me to be here for it."

I sip coffee and cradle the mug. "I may look calm, but inside, I'm nervous."

He nods. "You wear it well."

"Time for breakfast." I whip up batter, pour it into a waffle maker, and pull them out just in time. There's talk that the first waffle isn't the best one, but I disagree. I think they're all tasty. We dig forks and knives into crisp waffles with maple syrup.

Someone knocks at the door, and my daughter Rose comes in with Max, my grandson. She says, "Are we too late for breakfast? It smells delicious."

I hug her and gesture to the kitchen. "Come join us.

There's more than enough for everyone. If we run out, I'll make more,"

Max bounces in place. "I want two waffles, with syrup."

I ruffle his mop of brown hair. "Why don't you take Buddy out in the back yard and run around while I make your waffles?"

He runs outside with Buddy, and my heart warms to see him. After breakfast, others arrive, and by the time we're out in the yard for the ashes ceremony, I look around the gathered group and smile at Jenna, Karina, Irena, Violet, Fred, Mary, Bernice, Mercury, Rose and Max, who have shown up to support me.

Yesterday, I dug a hole in the back yard and prepared the soil. Taking a spade in my hands, I stand in the mist, dressed in a black puffer jacket and a black wool watch cap, and say, "Thank you for joining in, as we bury Albert's ashes and remember the best parts of him. He was a loving father and husband and an excellent business owner, and I wish he had lived much longer. But we can't change the past or direct when death comes, so after a difficult year, I'm finally ready to bury his ashes along with his favorite plant, the pink peony. We'll plant the peony, and then I'd like to say a few more words. Rose, would you like to say something?"

She says, "No, just that he was a really good father, and I miss him every day."

I place the peony in the hole I dug, sprinkle in the

container of ashes and add soil on top of that. I say, "Max, would you like to do the honors and water it?"

He nods and picks up a watering can, pouring water on overturned soil around the plant. When he's finished, and the can is empty, I clear my throat. "And now let's talk about turning to the future and looking ahead. You were all aware of my efforts to build Stone Estates on a hill above town. But I'd like to announce that as part of my moving on and building a new future for myself, I'm giving up my husband's plans for Stone Estates, and I'm creating a new dream, one that will be more environmentally friendly and fit in better with the community. I'll build tiny homes instead, with a big dog park, and Buddy can go there and have the time of his life, along with humans."

Bernice raises her eyebrows sky high. Fred runs a hand through his thinning hair. Mary grins, and Irena nods and smiles, as do others. Thinking back on the difficulties I've come through to stand in this place today, I say, "Thank you for your support this past year. I appreciate you. Any questions?"

"Tell us more about the park," Irena says, raising her hand.

"I thought we'd have a trail, where people could sit on benches and look west over the water to the San Juan Islands, enjoying the view, when they're not walking with their dogs."

Everyone nods. Mary says, "That sounds good."

Bernice says, "Great idea. The town needs it, and we're behind you one-hundred percent."

"Way to adjust under pressure and flex," Fred says. "I'm impressed."

We tromp in the house and share stories over cups of coffee, tea and sparkling cider, along with cheese and crackers. I smile and look around the room, knowing I'm lucky to have such good friends and loving family.

I sidle up to Rose and say, "I hope you don't mind that I didn't bring your brother today from Shore Lodge to see your father's ashes buried?"

My daughter wrinkles her nose. "I didn't want him here. He'd find a way to make the event about him, and he'd be angry about something. Besides, I called Shore Lodge and it sounds like he's pretty out of it."

I give her a hug, and she holds me tight. "I love you, dear one."

She pats my back. "Love you too, Mom."

Stepping away, I say, "I just have one more thing to do in the coming days, and that is to pay a visit to Dusty at Shore Lodge. Do you want to go?"

She makes a face. "I'd rather not. It's his fault he's there, and his body is compromised. He shouldn't have gone into the mountains when there were avalanche warnings. Like always, he thought he knew better than the experts. Besides, I have work to do and can't leave Seattle for a while."

A few hours later, I say goodbye to my guests,

including Rose and Max, who head back to Seattle. Mercury and I wash the dishes and clean the kitchen. Turning to him, I say, "It feels good to have a helper to clean up this mess. Thanks for hanging around."

He leans the broom handle against the counter and opens his arms. A wide smile spread across my face as I step close and wrap my arms around him. He hums, and we gently sway to a tune no one else can hear.

He pats my back. "This is the life, isn't it?"

I lean into his warm chest and listen to his heart beat, sure and steady. "It sure is."

JENNA

Returning from Jacklyn's event, where she buried her husband's ashes, I stand in my living room and stare into the house next door. My husband and Zoila have been cooped up next door for days, only opening the front door to accept food deliveries. I've closed our joint credit card accounts and contacted the major credit agencies to freeze my credit, in case Zoila or Kirk try to take out a loan or open a new credit card in my name.

When my phone dings with a message, I check it, and my eyebrows shoot up when I see it's from Zoila. She wrote, 'I have information about Kirk that he doesn't want you to know. I'll tell you what it is for fifty thousand dollars. Pay in cash, and you have twenty-four hours to deliver it. Don't tell Kirk about this.'

I snort. She's an idiot to think I'd be a sucker and fall

for that. Who cares what Kirk's secret is? I don't. It's too late to save our marriage, which met a sudden death when Zoila stepped between us and drained our funds.

I text back. 'No. Besides, it's Saturday. You can't get that much cash in twenty-four hours. Maybe I'll tell the cops what you're up to.'

She replies, 'It's not fair you kicked us out. I'm supposed to be healing, but you created a negative environment. Can you loan me a thousand dollars?'

'No. Go away. Get out of my life'

I turn off my phone and make chicken enchiladas for dinner. An hour later, sirens grow louder, coming closer. I stride over to the front window and look out. A police car pulls up with flashing lights next door, and Zoila lets them in. Officers lead Kirk out in handcuffs, put him in the back of the squad car and drive away.

Zoila waves to me from her living room, and my pulse picks up. I pull the blinds closed, shutting her out of my life. If I even blink at her, she'll be over here like a shot, knocking on the door, asking for anything that's not nailed down.

I race around inside my house, locking doors and throwing deadbolts out of caution. I lock the windows to prevent Zoila from climbing inside and creeping around.

Ten minutes later, Zoila knocks on the front door. I frown, because she might have Kirk's key and let herself in. I'll have to get the locks changed. She rings the bell and knocks again. "Let me in. We need to talk. Let's band together and work against him."

"Go away. Get out of my life. If you don't leave, I'll call the cops and report you for trespassing.'

She shuffles away, and I call the man who owns the house next door. "I need to tell you something about your house. The rent for the woman living there was paid by my husband, Kirk, but he was just arrested, and he won't be able to pay rent. You might have a hard time getting Zoila, the woman in your home, to move out."

52

KIRK

I'm booked into jail and read my rights. For my one phone call, I reach out to Jenna. When she picks up, I say, "Jenna, I'm so sorry for what happened. I could've been kinder and not caved to what Zoila wanted. But they arrested me, and I need you to bail me out."

"What did they charge you with?"

"Embezzling funds."

"From where?"

I cringe. "From a hot tub company and the place I work now."

"We're through. I'll serve you divorce papers in jail, and you'd better sign if you know what's good for you."

"Wait, you don't understand," but she hangs up, and I frown at a dead dial tone.

An officer says, "Back to the cells for you."

My armpits are damp with sweat. My body odor reeks

of fear. "Wait, I need to call someone else. I know an attorney."

He shakes his head. "That was your one call. You should've thought of that first." He slaps handcuffs on my wrists and marches me to a jail cell. "Let me guess, you called your wife, and she told you to get lost?"

"Yeah, but I'm innocent. I just need to prove it. Once I'm bailed out, I'll prove the charges are wrong. The woman who called the police on me is a known liar. You can't trust what she says."

He chuckles. "Losers like you don't get it. It wasn't only her. You current employer suspected you of embezzling money from the company. You'd better get used to being treated like a criminal, because you'll be in prison for a long time."

The jail cell door slams shut, and I sit on a hard bench, resting my head in my hands. Before the cops showed up and took me away, I said to Zoila, "Is it true? Did you lie to me about being sick? Did you take my money, but you don't have cancer?"

She said in a matter-of-fact voice, "Yes, I did. I took your money and faked having cancer, and I got away with it."

I blinked and realized I'd made a terrible mistake by not believing Jenna and folding to Zoila's demands. I'd picked the wrong person to side with, and she was without a conscience. That was when I knew I was through with her. How twisted was her mind to think up these lies and tell them in such a convincing manner?

I swore at her, and I yelled. "You tricked me, and you lied. You were fine the whole time? I can't believe how gullible I was."

I expected her to apologize and beg for my forgiveness, but she smiled and took out her phone. She reported me to the police for embezzling and threw away my life forever. From here on out, I'll be lucky to see sunlight.

53

ZOILA

The landline rings, and I pick it up, full of hope that Jenna changed her mind and decided to team up together against Kirk to bring him down. "Hello?"

"Hi, we're the owners of the home you've been renting, and you need to move out right now. We're coming back tonight. If you don't vacate the premises in the next thirty minutes, leaving it spotless, I'll report you to the police for fraudulent activities."

"Fraudulent? I haven't done anything wrong. Besides, I'm not leaving. Kirk paid the next month's rent in advance."

"Actually, you're wrong about that. He didn't pay, and he told us to come back anytime and that you'd be living next door in Jenna's house. But she informed me that isn't true. She said you've been coercing Kirk into giving you money."

"But I need to live here. I'm sick. Haven't you heard?"

"Whatever reasons you have for scamming him, you'd better leave town right now. I have friends who are attorneys who will hunt you down and send you to jail for what you did to Jenna."

"I can't move that fast. It's impossible. I have a lot to pack. I'll be out in a month, that's the earliest I can manage."

He says in a deep voice, "This isn't up to you. You've milked the system long enough. You have a choice. Leave Millersville right now with the shirt on your back, or stay and go to jail. You'll rot in there for a long time."

My palms go cold. "I'm innocent. You can't talk to me this way. It's an outrage."

He sighs. "Jenna told me you'd be difficult. Listen, leave, or we'll toss you to the curb. I'm sure the neighbors would be glad to help oust you from our house. One hour is all you have to drive past the city limits and never come back to town. If I ever see you in Millersville, I'll black ball your name to every person in town. I'll make your life miserable. Get. Out. Of. My. House. Now."

He hangs up, and I fling the phone down, screaming. My heart races. He meant what he said, I could tell. I'd better take him seriously and leave. I don't want to be thrown in jail.

I run upstairs, throw clothes in a suitcase and toss the

wig I don't need in the trash. Goodbye, Millersville. I blew up Jenna and Kirk's marriage, so I achieved my primary goal of punishing them for what they did to me.

I step outside, hands trembling, and open Jenna's car, placing my suitcase and purse in the car. Inserting Kirk's car key in the ignition, I start it and drive away. Jenna runs out of the house, shaking a fist and yelling, but I drive down the block, laughing to myself. I'm headed to the next town, where I'll find another target, and another one after that. I could drive south into Oregon and ply my trade in Eugene, a college town.

I'm about to cross Jackson Bridge, when a police car approaches with flashing lights. I stomp on the accelerator and fly down the road, but the police car sticks with me, siren wailing. With a sigh, I pull off on a dirt road and roll down my window.

The officer approaches, and I smile, pulling my blouse a little bit lower. "Sorry, officer, I didn't mean to speed back there. I'll be more careful in the future."

He asks for my vehicle registration and driver's license. My heart races, and I run a hand over my stubbled scalp, forcing a smile. "I've been very ill from having cancer, and my brain is fried from chemotherapy. Could you please just let me off with a warning, pretty please?"

"I'm going to ask you to get out of the car with your hands above your head."

I tilt my head. "Surely, you can't mean that, Officer. I was only going a tiny bit over the speed limit."

He frowns. "Ma'am, get out of the car now. Don't make this situation worse than it is.

With a shrug, I run through ideas in my mind, plotting how to get myself out of this scrape. My super-strength of manipulating people failed me, when it mattered most. I don't want to go to jail, and I've got to leave Millersville behind.

I bite my lip and nod. He isn't responding to my flirting and begging, so I take a radical step. "Hold on, it'll take me a few minutes. The cancer meds made me weak and muddled my brain."

In the space of a few seconds, I open my purse and pull out a pistol, aiming it at him. The gun is heavy in my hand, but I hold it steady. "Let me go, or I'll shoot you."

"You don't want to do that. This won't end well."

"Let me go, or you'll regret it."

Crickets sound in the still moment between my freedom and jail. Before I can pull the trigger, he knocks the gun out of my hand, opens the door and yanks me out of the car, handcuffing me.

I scream and scuffle, resisting with all my might, but he drags me to the squad car and stuffs me in the back, reading me my rights.

Tears stream down my face, and I say, "Stop. Don't do this. Let me go."

He drives away, with me in the back, wailing.

He says, "The car has been reported stolen, and you just threatened an officer."

"My friend said I could borrow the car whenever I wanted."

"Tell it to someone else."

He takes me into jail, where I'm booked. I use my one phone call to call Jenna, pleading for help, but she doesn't pick up. I have no one else to turn to.

A female officer shows me to a cell and locks me inside. My cellmate is a drunk woman with pungent body odor. I grab the cold metal bars and yell, "Get me out. I'm sick. I shouldn't be in jail." But no one comes.

"I want dinner. I deserve food. Bring me high-protein, non-gluten pasta with olive oil and broccoli florets."

The drunk lady in the cell cackles. "Nice try, baldie. What're you in for?"

"I have no idea. I'm innocent."

She burps, and a stale odor of beer makes me wrinkle my nose. This never should have happened. My mistake was believing Kirk when he said his wife was laid back and would swallow lies he fed her. Our scheme to defraud her and drain her funds flopped. If I ever see him again, I'll throttle him for causing my downfall.

I rattle the bars and yell, "I want a different cell, all by myself."

No one comes to my aid. I've always gotten my way until now, but it doesn't appear my sex appeal is working in my favor. I'm not sure what to do.

My cellmate vomits into a bucket and wipes her

mouth. The air fills with the putrid odor of puke, and I breathe through my mouth. This is far worse than I imagined in nightmares about getting caught by the cops.

She says, "You know how to get them to reduce the charges, don't you?"

"No, how?"

"Blame it on someone else, before they pin it on you."

I nod. "That's a good idea, thanks."

And suddenly, I know what to do. I'll tell my court-appointed lawyer and anyone else who will listen that Kirk was the master mind behind the plan to defraud Jenna. He was the one who manipulated me and convinced me to take Jenna's car to sell it in another town and turn the money over to him.

A smile spreads across my face. It's a simple story of deflection, and I think they'll buy it. The road ahead will be less bumpy than I imagined when I walked through the jail doors. "You may have saved me," I say. "I appreciate it."

"Here's your first lesson. Don't say thanks to anyone in jail or prison, or you'll be in their debt forever. And another thing. Keep your mouth shut."

I close my mouth, and for the first time in my life, I don't try to milk something out of another person for my benefit. My plan is to tell the lawyers and judge that I was abandoned by my husband, and Kirk plotted against his wife, aiming to drain her of money and get her to move out, leaving the house to him. Armed with these lies, I'll convince them to release me, and I'll start over in a new place.

54

IRENA

I let myself into the house that was left to me and sniff the air, detecting a clean home washed of decay and death. I empty the dishwasher, putting away bowls and mugs, and whistle while I work. I wonder how Kelly is doing and decide to call her at dinnertime.

Heavy footsteps clomp up the back steps, and I freeze. Tiptoeing over, I look out the kitchen window, but don't see anyone. Being in this house suddenly feels wrong. I don't belong here. This was my friend's place.

My heart pounds, and a thick glass mug slips out of my slick hands, falling to the floor with a thud, but it doesn't break. Picking it up, I flinch when someone knocks hard on the door four times.

I hurry to the door and glance outside at a haggard man with a lined face and long shaggy hair. He says in a hoarse voice, "Can I come in?"

"No, I'm the new owner. Please go away."

"I was sent here to talk to you about Buzz."

I shake my head. "I don't believe you. Go away, or I'll call the police."

He turns the door knob to enter, but I locked the door when I came in out of an abundance of caution. He says in a gruff voice, "You'll want to hear what I have to say."

I pull out my phone and start to dial the police, but he looks up, pushes a strand of hair out of his face, and our eyes lock.

A wild thought runs through my mind, and I shake my head. They never found his body, so what if Buzz is alive and came home? But that's impossible. This man looks nothing like our longtime friend who lied to us. He's dead.

"Irena," he says. "It's me, back from the dead."

Goosebumps prick my flesh, and I gasp.

His voice is less raspy when he says, "It's true, I'm Buzz."

Recognizing his voice, I throw open the door and give him a quick hug. But I remember how he hurt Jack, and I step back. Fiddling with my fingers, I say, "I didn't recognize you. I can't believe you're alive. What happened?"

He shrugs. "It's a wild story, but an old woman rescued me when I washed up on shore. She brought me back to life in a shack by the water, and it took months for me to heal. I can't believe I survived the fall from the bridge."

I shiver and cross my arms. "It's weird to see you. If you weren't standing here, I wouldn't believe it. Of course, you'll want your house back, and the boat, and the bookstore. I cleaned the house and tossed out the moldy food, so it's ready for you to move in. Oh, and your employees own the bookstore now, with a cut to me. And your boat is where you left it. I didn't decide what to do with it yet."

He runs a hand down over his face. "I'm been doing a lot of thinking, and I think it's best for me to move on. Let's just pretend you never saw me. I've caused too much pain for others, especially Jack. If I stayed in town, I'd only be a bad reminder of the past. They might arrest me and put me in prison for almost killing Jack, even though it was a mistake. I didn't mean to hurt him so bad."

My throat clogs with tears. "You left him bleeding by the wharf and didn't call for help. How could you do that? He's really messed up from the injury you caused, when he fell back and hurt his head. I can't believe you did that. Everything I knew about you was a lie."

He says in a low voice, "It was a mistake I wish I hadn't made in a flash of rage. I was jealous of him and how you still loved him."

My hands clench. "He's the father of my child. Of course, I still care about him. You almost ripped Kelly's father from her life. I think it's best if you move on. Maybe I should call the cops."

He sighs. "Please don't do that. I'll be out of your life in no time, and they'll never know I was here."

I tap a toe, wondering what to do. I happened to be at his house when he stopped by, so I could just pretend I never saw him and never tell another soul. Can I carry that secret to my grave and be responsible for Jack not getting justice for almost dying by this man's hand?

He says, "Look, I'm only here for a few minutes. I'm moving on to a new place, where I'll start over. Please don't report me. Let them think I was dead."

I run a finger over my lips, torn between loyalty to my longest friend and reporting him to the police. "You grew up here, with so many friends. It won't be easy to go somewhere new."

He studies me. "If I stayed and did a stint in prison, no one would talk to me, given what I did to Jack. Believe me, I wish I could take back those moments when I hit Jack in a fury. I'd do anything to relive that and do it differently. My deepest regret is how I let my temper take over, and I almost killed my best friend. Do you believe me? I know I did the wrong thing, but I can't think of a way to make it right to him."

His eyes fill with tears, and I nod, saying, "I believe you."

In a rough voice, he says, "I stopped by their new place and looked in the window. He and Abby look pretty messed up. Was she in an accident or something? How did she get hurt?"

"She was driving in a snowstorm on I-5, trying to get to Kelly, who was kidnapped."

His eyes grow wide. "Poor Kelly. How is she?"

I swallow tears. "She's on Grand Island, going to

school there for a bit, to get away from kids in town who bullied her."

"I'm sorry to hear about that. I'd better get on my way."

"Where are you going?"

"I'm not sure, but before I go, I have one request. Would it be all right with you if I took the framed picture of you and the leather journal from the closet in the second bedroom?"

I tilt my head. "That's fine. I didn't get a chance to read the poems. Take whatever you want. It's your house."

"Not anymore. I deserve to be stripped of my earthly possessions after I let my temper get the better of me and unleased my fury on my best friend. Besides, the poems weren't meant to be read by you or anyone else. They're letters from my soul and a cry for love."

"I'm sorry it didn't work out between us."

"I'll find true love one day, but it might not be in this lifetime."

I wince at how sad he sounds and change the subject. "Do you want your car?"

He nods. "I was hoping to get it back. Is that possible?"

I grab the car keys off a hook and hand them to him. His fingernails are dirty, his hands are calloused, and his are not the bookseller's hands that once held me.

I say, "It's yours, but I think you might need to add gas." I think about offering to cook a meal for him before he goes on his way, but I quickly jettison that idea. It's better for both of us if he leaves right away. Seeing him dredges up painful memories of when Buzz fed me lies about Jack's whereabouts, after he went missing off our friend's boat.

He says, "I'll get those items and be on my way. Keep doing what you were doing, and I'll grab some clothes and load the car. You can sell my boat, or give it to Kelly when she's older. She might like that. She always was a great first mate."

A tear trickles down my cheek. "She'll be sorry she missed seeing you."

He puts a finger to his lips. "Don't tell her I was here. Let her think of me as dead. By the way, I never told you, but I was jealous when you married Jack, and you had a baby with him. I used to pretend you and I were Kelly's parents. That made me happy."

I wipe my eyes, not daring to say a word. If I speak, I'll break down sobbing. I don't love him anymore except in a platonic way, but all my mixed emotions about Jack going missing and Buzz deceiving me are brought to the surface with his return.

"I'll be on my way then. Let's say goodbye now, so I can just go when the car is packed. It'll be easier that way."

We hug, and I let go first. He's thin, and I can feel his ribs. "Bye, Buzz."

"Bye, gorgeous. I'll never forget you."

I swallow hard. "Tell you what, I'll leave and come back later. Lock up when you leave, okay?"

"Sure, I will. We were good together, don't you think?"

I smile through tears. "Most of the time. Thanks for being my friend when I was new to town and the weird girl from east of the mountains with no father."

He smiles. "I'll always be there for you, Irena, and I'll keep the same cell phone number, in case you want to call. Let me know if you ever change your mind about us."

"Goodbye." I pick up my purse and stumble out to my car, starting it and driving away in a daze. Like many times before when something is bothering me, I end up on my boat to mull things over. I check the oil, warm up the engine and putter out of the marina to soothe my soul with splashing waves and the rocking of the boat. I've found my calling in being a mother and rescuing boaters in distress, but I haven't yet had a longtime love go the distance.

On instinct, I navigate west through Cedar Channel, across Rosario Strait and make my way toward Grand Island to see my daughter, the most important person in my life. I don't think I'll tell her I saw Buzz. That news would be difficult for her to absorb with all she's processing after being abducted. I definitely will not tell Abby and Jack that Buzz is alive, because that would unnerve them and possibly slow their recovery from injuries. I suppose I can keep a secret like that for the rest of my life, if it helps protect my loved ones. I want to help Kelly, Jack and Abby heal from trauma, so we can go back to being the best group of people around, laughing and listening and sharing meals with each other. It might take a long time to get there, but I think we can do it.

I text Kelly and Tex saying I'm on my way and pocket my phone. I push on the throttle to increase my speed, ploughing through waves and heading to my wonderful daughter.

55
____

KELLY

I'm home from school on Grand Island, eating vanilla yogurt with homemade strawberry jam. Tex said she made the jam last summer, and I can help her next summer, if I hang around and don't go home over the summer. A tug of sadness pulls at my heart, because I miss my mom and dad.

My phone dings with a text, and I grin when I see Mom is due to arrive soon. I finish the bowl of yogurt, gulp down a glass of water and put the dishes in the dishwasher, like Tex asked me to. I grab my rain jacket and run out into the mist to help Mom tie up the boat when she arrives.

Waves lap the shore and dock pilings. Mom's boat comes around the bend, and my pulse picks up. I wave to her, and she waves back, sounding the horn.

She pulls up to the dock, and I tie her dock lines. I

wait for her to disembark, and before I know it, she's on the dock, wrapping me in her strong arms.

I hold on to her, smelling her sea-scented hair, and she says, "I've missed you so much. Tell me everything that's going on."

We walk side by side up the paved road to Tex's house, and when Mom and I enter and Tex greets us, my world feels whole again. We sit down at the table with drinks, water for me, coffee for Mom and tea for Tex, and I babble about my new school and hikes I've taken with kids on the island.

Mom says, "Are you feeling any better? I know it'll take a while, but I just wanted to check."

I smile. "Yeah, I'm feeling better, away from kids who judged me but don't know what I went through or who I became on the other side. I'm glad I made the change, and thank you, Tex, for letting me stay here."

Mom turns to Tex. "Yes, thanks. We really appreciate you having her live here for the rest of the school year."

My eyebrows go up. "I was hoping to stay over the summer and next year too for school."

Tex says, "That would be fine with me, as long as you obey my rules."

Mom frowns. "We'll talk about it later."

I groan. "That always means no."

Mom tilts her head and smiles. "Maybe not this time. I'm learning new habits."

Tex grins. "Aren't we all?"

56

JACKLYN

The next day, Mercury and I stand at the front window, drinking coffee and watching rain come down. Sipping coffee, I say, "So much happened in the last year, you'd think it would be a blur, but every detail is crisp and clear in my mind."

"I'll bet. I suspect we relive traumatic events like seeing a movie flash through our minds, until you can tell the story differently to yourself."

I nod. "I'm working on that. Part of changing how I view my story involves not fearing my son, not reacting to his temper flares and ignoring him when he tries to finagle money from me. I've decided it's time I visited Dusty at Shore Lodge. It's been long enough."

Cradling a coffee cup, he says, "I'll go with you to Cedar Island, if you like."

I shake my head and bend to pet Buddy, who licks my

hand. "Thanks, but I have to do this on my own. If Nurse Wright gives me any guff, I'll look her in the eyes and tell her to stuff it. But I've got to see how Dusty is doing. Walking the halls of Shore Lodge will be facing down a nightmare and rejiggering my past."

"Too bad Rose couldn't go with you," he says, shoving a hand in his pocket.

I shrug. "I don't think she wanted to, and she has to be in Seattle for work. She says Dusty is lucky to be alive, and he brought it on himself by ignoring avalanche warnings and not checking changing weather conditions."

He says, "Everyone wants to assign blame when tragedy strikes. It's a human tendency to climb on the blame train, instead of finding a way to fix things, so it won't happen again."

I kiss his cheek and go into the kitchen, leaving my coffee cup in the sink. Zipping up my puffer jacket, I pick up my purse and glance outside, where slanting rain is pouring down. "I'm not sure if there's a fix for Dusty's attitude of entitlement. And I doubt he feels lucky to be alive, despite what Rose said. Can you imagine not being able to walk or talk?"

Mercury smiles, adjusting a purple polka dot bow tie clipped to his long gray beard. "You'd shrivel up and die if you couldn't talk, take Buddy on walks and stop to chat with everyone you see."

I cock my head. "I do have a tendency to blather on at times."

He gives me a kiss on the lips and steps back, gesturing to the door. "I'm enjoying every minute of the ride, but you'd better leave now, before you miss the ferry."

I say goodbye and rush out the door, pulling up my hood in the pelting rain as I make my way to the garage. Driving away to the ferry, I gnaw on my lower lip, wondering what it will feel like to be back in the facility where my son admitted me for all time. But now the tables are turned, and he's the one who is locked inside.

I get in line for the ferry and, while I wait, I call Shore Lodge to confirm I'm coming to visit my son. A charge nurse says, "It will be good for him to see you. He hasn't had any visitors yet, and he's taking tentative steps, using a walker."

"I'm glad to hear that." We say goodbye and hang up, but I frown. Part of me doesn't want my son to recover his full abilities, because that would mean he'd return to this side of the channel, and he'd be back to cooking up ways to take my money.

The ferry arrives, and black smoke billows out of a smokestack. Cars, trucks, bicyclists and people walking off the boat depart for various destinations, each of them probably thinking what they're doing is the most important task.

A ferry worker in an orange vest waves me ahead, and I drive on the little twenty-eight car ferry. I roll down the window, shut off the car and take a deep breath of salt air.

Glancing ahead as the boat takes off, engine whirring, I sigh, marveling at how life changes, with ebbs and flow and twists and turns. We never know where it's going, even when we think we do. We can plan, but in the end something happens, and we must adjust and learn to adapt.

The ferry bumps into the dock on the Cedar Island side, lines are secured, the gates goes up, and we depart. My stomach knots as I drive up a gravel lane to Shore Lodge. My armpits prick with sweat.

I park by the two-story building, which appears inviting, but those on the inside know the windows and doors are locked. No one can leave without authorization, but I escaped. Turning off the car, I lean back and say to myself, "Nurse Wright isn't an all-powerful wizard, and she can't control me. I'll be fine. I'll go in, get out and go home. No problem."

I stride inside to the reception desk, pulse pounding in my ears, feeling I was most fortunate to make it home one dark night from this prison of a place. "Hello, I'm here to visit my son, Dusty Stone, on the second floor."

She smiles. "Certainly. Sign in please, and wait over there. Someone will be with you soon to escort you up to the secure second floor."

I sign in, and she says, "Have you seen our secure psychiatric ward before? Because if not, what you see and hear might surprise you. Be prepared for unusual behaviors from our residents."

I break into a coughing fit, covering my mouth. Leaning on the counter, I say, "Yes, I've been up there before. I was mistakenly admitted by a family member, but I managed to get out and reclaim my life and rescue my dog from the shelter before it was too late."

Her mouth drops open. "Oh, gosh, well, I don't know what to say, except that's great you recovered from whatever was bothering you. You look fine to me."

I smile. "I'm better than fine. My greedy son wanted my money, but I closed the financial spigot, you might say. All is fine for me now. For him, not so much. Whatever you do, don't go out in the mountains when there are avalanche warnings, like Dusty did. He's recovering upstairs."

I close my mouth because I've been rambling on too long.

She reaches out and pats the counter. "It sounds like you've been through a lot, and I'm glad you got well."

"Thank you." I turn away to stand by a window, feeling too nervous to sit down, and look over a meadow, where plants wave back and forth in the wind. Beyond the meadow is Cedar Channel, where boats bounce in white caps. I cross my fingers and hope coming to see Dusty wasn't a mistake. Of course he'd like a visitor, because I did when I was entombed in the stark, sterile unit, until he cut me off from seeing my friends.

A young woman fresh out of high school with her hair

in a ponytail exits the elevator and walks toward me. "Jacklyn Stone?"

My hands tremble. "Yes."

"Right this way."

On the ride in the elevator going up to the secure second floor, I rest a hand on my churning stomach. I shouldn't have come. Reliving a nightmare is a mistake.

The elevator door opens, and we step off. She holds her badge up to a device on the wall, and the sliding glass doors open. An overwhelming odor of lemon-scented cleansers with an undertone of urine wafts out, and I wrinkle my nose.

An older gray-haired woman in a floral housedress shuffles up to the sliding glass doors with a purse hanging on her arm. She says, "I have to go shopping to make dinner."

The aide says to the resident, "Let's go back to the dayroom."

The three of us slowly make our way down the hall. The older woman turns to go into a room, and we continue on. The walls are white. Our shoes squeak on the linoleum floor. Florescent overhead lights cast an eerie glow.

The aide stops outside the dayroom, and I peer inside, spotting my son. I force a smile.

The aide says to me, "Don't get too close, for your own safety. He's been angry and lashing out. You can go in now."

She stands in the doorway, and I spot my friend Florence and wave to her. Her bird's nest of a red wig is slightly askew, and she gets up, wrapping me in her arms. My friends Grit and Billy, who I met during my stay here, do the same. I grin. "You look beautiful, as always."

Billy whispers, "Is that your son over there?"

"Yes," I say in a low voice. "Can you believe it? I'd better go visit him"

From across the room, Dusty clenches his jaw, glaring at me. A vein throbs in his forehead. His face is flushed, and I nod, knowing this look well. I glance behind me to make sure the aide on duty is in the doorway, although that wisp of a girl won't be able to stop my son's mighty fury, if he unleashes it.

When I take a step toward Dusty, he stands on shaking legs and lifts his walker, throwing it across the room. It smashes into the television. Cracks appear, the screen goes dark, and residents groan.

Two burly, muscled male aides in white rush in to subdue my son. Nurse Wright sweeps in and administers a shot in his arm. Dusty looks at me with glazed eyes, and the aides march Dusty out, lock step.

Nurse Wright turns on me full force, with her hands on her hips, eyes ablaze. "He was calm until you arrived. You need to leave right now. You're upsetting the residents, and I won't allow that. You're a trouble-maker. No wonder your son acted out."

I stand tall, arms at my sides, and face the mighty

mountain of the woman in charge of this secure ward. I say in a steady, clear voice, "I am and will always be calm at my core. This environment unnerved me, as it would for any sane person admitted against her will by a family member. I'll leave now, but I'll be back. You can bet on that."

I wave goodbye to my friends. "Bye. See you later. Love you."

"Love you too," Grit calls.

I walk out the door and head back to my yellow bungalow, the best dog in the world, my new friend Mercury, my beautiful life and my bright future.

Next up is *The Gas Station Motel,* Book 5 in the series.

A nightmare waits for her at a motel in the middle of nowhere. When Jacklyn's niece stops at a remote motel overnight, she wakes up in a strange, sterile room. Members of a crime ring are about to harvest her kidney to sell on the black market. Jacklyn, who has her own challenges, realizes something is wrong, and she runs to the rescue.

Thank you for reading *These Lies*! Please let other readers know what to expect by posting ratings and reviews on Goodreads, Amazon and BookBub.

Don't miss out on book reviews and book deals! Subscribe to my author newsletter
On my website: www.susanspechtoram.com

Follow me on BookBub for updates

My Facebook author page is Susan Specht Oram Author

If you're on YouTube, check out my channel @susanspechtoramauthor

Thank you for reading my books!

ABOUT THE AUTHOR

Susan is writing mysteries-thrillers and creative nonfiction. Previously, she served as senior director of corporate communications for biotechnology companies. Susan worked as an activity aide in an upscale nursing home's secure psychiatric unit. She was a potter and painter with an art studio in Seattle and has also worked as a market researcher, a nurse's aide, a waitress, and a library page. Her essays have been published in Mothering Magazine, Twins Magazine and Utne Reader. Susan grew up near Detroit, Michigan. She lives in a windy part of the Pacific Northwest with her husband and rescue dog.

Mysteries-Thrillers by Susan Specht Oram
Shore Lodge
The Thieves
Cabin Eight
Secrets at the Café
The Mother's Threat
Under Jackson Bridge
Missing Man
By Midnight

The Winter Storm
The Cold Night
Avalanche
These Lies
The Gas Station Motel

Creative Nonfiction: Strangers on a Train Series
Green Light
The Train
Canoe
Soup Kettle
Bathtub
Phone Call
Watering Can
Waterfall
Strangers on a Train Series collection (Books 1-8)

Humorous fiction:
Boating with Buddy, a report from a canine correspondent

Nonfiction:
Brief business books on investor relations, crisis communication and public relations